HOUSE OF ROT

DANGER SLATER

Cover Art by Kate Blairstone
Interior Illustrations by Echo Echo
Edited by Alex Woodroe

Production of this novel was made possible in part by a grant from the Regional Arts & Culture Council. Visit https://racc.org/ for more information.

Published by Tenebrous Press.
Visit our website at www.tenebrouspress.com.

First Printing, June 2023.

Print ISBN: 979-8-9859923-8-0
eBook ISBN: 979-8-9859923-9-7

Cover art by Kate Blairstone

Interior illustrations by Echo Echo.

Jacket design by Matt Blairstone.

Edited by Alex Woodroe.

Formatting by Lori Michelle.

ALSO FROM TENEBROUS PRESS:

Agony's Lodestone
a novella by Laura Keating

Soft Targets
a novella by Carson Winter

Crom Cruach
a novella by Valkyrie Loughcrewe

Lure
a novella by Tim McGregor

One Hand to Hold, One Hand to Carve
a novella by M.Shaw

Your Body is Not Your Body:
A Body Horror Anthology from Trans & Gender Nonconforming
Voices
edited by Alex Woodroe with Matt Blairstone

**Brave New Weird: The Best New Weird Horror,
Vol. One**
edited by Alex Woodroe with Matt Blairstone

More titles at www.TenebrousPress.com

To Constance

*"When life itself seems lunatic,
who knows where madness lies?"*

—Miguel de Cervantes, *Don Quixote*

FIRST NIGHT

AND
THEN
THERE
WERE
FOOTSTEPS

I

All was silent.

And then there were footsteps.

Lithe and limber. One after another. The sound of gummy bare soles sticking to the freshly-lacquered wood, skulking around the apartment, almost as steady as a metronome. The living room. The kitchen. Up and down the hall. Not a single floorboard remained uncreaked.

Elenya DeNova opened her eyes. A full moon peeked through the slats in the blinds, casting a pale light like prison bars on the opposite wall. Aside from that, there was only darkness.

The footsteps continued into the bathroom. Whoever was out there was in no hurry to leave. They knocked around like they owned the place, rattling door handles, rummaging around in the closets. The pipes gurgled and the water swirled. *Waloooooshhh glughglughglugh.* Yes, someone was using their toilet. Someone was tapping on their walls. Someone was shuffling about.

Myles stirred but didn't rouse. Elenya could hear the sound of his breath as he exhaled through his nose. She could feel the heat of his body trapped with her beneath the sheets. The two of them in bed together. Peas in a pod.

The mattress they slept on they bought just a week prior, at the Mattress Factory Outlet. There'd been so many options to choose from. A showroom full of options. But this was the one. They knew this was the one. It was made out of that high-tech memory foam stuff. That NASA stuff. The good stuff. When laid upon, it would conform to the exact size and shape of your body. Soothing and soft and ameliorative. Go ahead. Close your eyes. Give 'er a spin. Let this state-of-the-art mattress into your heart. Let it embrace you with its mother-like hug.

DANGER SLATER

The mattress arrived yesterday, the same exact day the DeNovas moved in. The UPS driver dropped it on their front doorstep, rolled up and vacuum-sealed in a box the size of a child's coffin. Once removed from the plastic, it would quickly expand, taking on more mattress-like dimensions as it doubled and tripled and quadrupled in size—a California King—so goddamn comfortable and convenient it made every other mattress they ever slept on look like complete and utter horseshit.

Between the security deposit and the U-Haul rental they'd nearly wiped out what meager savings they had. Times were tough for the newlywed couple. Nothing was cheap, not even the gas it took to get there. Sacrifice was the name of the game. They cut back on the avocado toast and learned to mix their own mimosas, and still, most financial experts would assuredly agree, a fancy new mattress was the exact type of extravagance neither of these two millennials could afford if they ever hoped to retire.

But even millennials needed to sleep on *something*, didn't they? And the weekend the DeNovas went bed shopping just so happened to be Memorial Day weekend as well, and the salesman at the store kept reassuring them that this was the BEST time to buy a new mattress. The ONLY time to buy a new mattress. When it came to the mattress industry, he said, Memorial Day was like their Christmas. All the BIG SALES and BLOWOUT DEALS would only last through Monday, he said, and there was no better way to honor the legacy of your fallen brothers-and-sisters-in-arms than to purchase THE VERY BEST piece of furniture you could from one of the big-box retailers out by the airport. After all, weren't these temporarily-reduced price points the kind of thing all those brave men and women fought and died for overseas?

"So why continue to punish yourself with those squeaky old springs and coils?" the salesman continued, his wrinkle-free discount store suit hanging too big on his slender frame. "You've worked hard and you've *earned* your rest, have you not? This space-age Silverflex™ memory foam mattress is literally the answer to all your dreams."

The DeNovas financed it on the spot—an 18-month payment plan for which they barely got approved. The interest rate was brutal, but they splurged anyway, justifying it as a wedding gift to themselves. Admittedly, it was not the most fiscally responsible purchase either of them ever made, but maybe, for once, do you think we could cut 'em a little slack? They'd already made so many concessions in the past. They'd already given up so much. And here they were, already in their mid-to-late 30s. Adults. And not even young adults either. Myles kept finding gray hairs in his chin stubble. Elenya could feel her biological clock quickly ticking down. They wanted to have babies one day. They wanted to start a family. They wanted to own a house. They wanted all those things. It didn't seem like too much to ask.

So, to the DeNovas, this wasn't just a mattress they slept on. It was a long-awaited promise that had finally been fulfilled.

Elenya shook her husband by the shoulder. "Myles. Myles, wake up."

Myles snorted himself awake. "Wh-what? What's wrong?"

Elenya put a finger to her lips, though it was too dark for him to tell.

"Shhh!"

"What?"

"I said *shhh*. Keep your voice down, Myles. Jeez-us!"

"Okay. Fine. I'm whispering. What's wrong?"

"There's someone in here."

"Huh?"

"There's someone else here. In the apartment."

"What are you talking about?"

"Don't talk. Just listen . . . "

They both paused. Didn't move. Didn't even breathe.

"I don't hear anything," he said after a few seconds.

"Shush! Listen closer."

They both held still again. This time, he heard it too. The donkey bray of their flimsy floorboards, echoing off the unadorned walls. Unmistakable. Someone was walking around out there. Down the hallway.

"Is it a robber?" asked Elenya.

"I don't think so," Myles replied. "Sounds to me like they're taking their sweet-ass time. If I was tryin'ta rob the place, I'd probably be a bit more discrete."

"What if it was the people who used to live here?"

"What do you mean?"

"Like the old tenants. The ones who lived here before us.

Maybe they got confused about where they lived now and came back to their old apartment instead of their new one."

"Don't they usually change the locks when people move out?"

"I think that might just be a thing landlords say. I don't think they bother unless there's a problem. Myles, there could be HUNDREDS of people with keys to this place."

"Okay, this is ridiculous." He was no longer bothering to whisper. "I'm gonna turn the lights on and go take a look."

He swung around and stood up. Elenya reached out and cried, "Myles, don't!" But she was already too late. He shuffled blindly across the room, bumping into the dresser before finding the far wall. This was only their first night and he still wasn't sure where all the furniture was yet. There were hidden hazards everywhere.

"C'mon, Ellie, think about it. Who could possibly be in here? What could they want? And why? We don't even own anything worth taking."

"What about the mattress?"

"Okay, sure, the mattress is worth a few bucks, but that'd be a pretty tricky heist to pull off, considering the fact that we're sleeping on top of it. Even if it's a robber, they're barking up the wrong tree. If they're lookin' for a big score, I'll just hafta kindly point them to the McMansions over by the outlet mall."

He flicked on the bedroom light, then turned on all the other lights in the apartment. Every light in every room. He even turned the brightness up on his phone and held it in front of him like a candelabra. Hell, if they owned a candelabra he would've lit that up too, leaving not a shadow for an intruder to hide.

The footsteps disappeared almost immediately, like someone hit the mute button on the remote control. *Click.* All of a sudden, there was silence once again.

Myles searched the apartment anyway. "We're still not alone," Elenya kept insisting. "I know we're not alone. I can FEEL it in the air."

"I can feel it in the air too," Myles concurred. "Like campfire smoke. Or a hot breath on the back of my neck."

They looked under the bed. In the back of the closet. Pulled back the shower curtain. Peeked behind the bathroom door. They even checked all the places it would be impossible for a person to hide. Beneath the couch cushions. Inside the refrigerator. Rolled up in a floor mat. Turning up nothing, except:

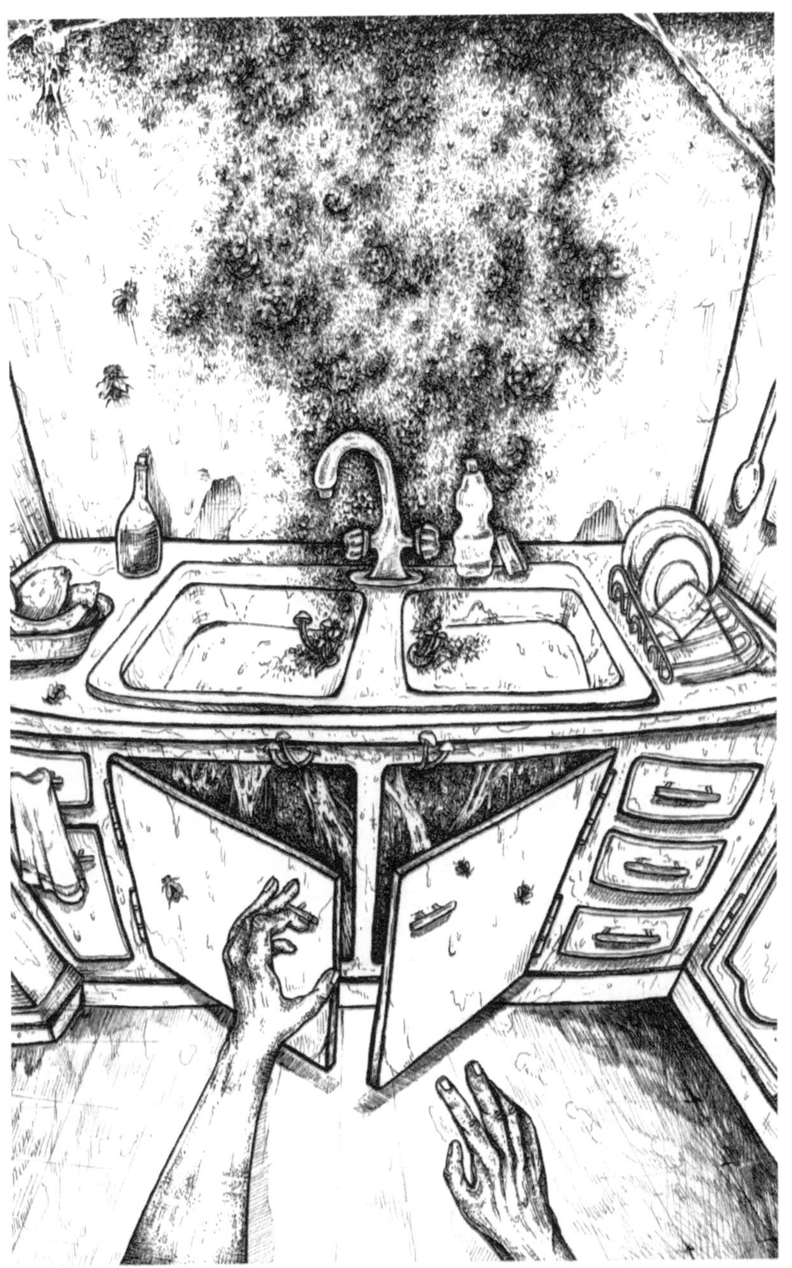

Growing unfettered for who knows how long, it had already overtaken the entire cabinet, and was now peeking out into the kitchen.

"Hey, Ellie, c'mere. Look at this."

She followed his voice to the kitchen. Myles had the cabinet open beneath the leaky sink. He stood back, arms crossed, and allowed her to look in.

"What the hell is that?" she said.

"I think it's black mold or something."

" . . . But it's not black."

"Okay, it's *very dark green* mold then."

"Is it toxic?"

"How would I know?"

"Looks like it's starting to spread." She leaned in closer. The mold branched out from the spot where the drainpipe fed into the wall. It was green and moist and mucusy on the bottom, white and fuzzy and filamentous on top. Two halves of a repulsive whole, swollen in the darkness.

"You know what they say about mold infestations, right? Once you can see it, it's already too late."

"Well, shit, let's hope that's not true."

Like a starburst, it covered the entire underside of the sink, almost in defiance of gravity itself. The slimy part appeared to work as a conveyance, a way for the mildew to get around, with the thin layer of fibrous fur resting on top like passengers aboard a jumbo jet. Splotchy and cadaverous. Tiny stalks twitching ever-so-slightly, the phalanges by which it explored the world.

Growing unfettered for who knows how long, it had already overtaken the entire cabinet, and was now peeking out into the kitchen. Fuzz turned to the light, as if seeing it for the first time. In awe.

"This is sick," said Elenya as she closed the door.

"No kidding. We'll clean it up in the morning. We'll make sure this whole place sparkles by the time we're done. But right now, we got bigger fish to fry."

"What are you thinking?"

"Honestly, babe? I don't know. I checked everywhere. You saw me, right? The front door and the windows are all locked from the inside. There are no trap doors in the floor. No secret passages in the walls. There ain't no way anyone is gettin' in or out of this apartment without us knowing about it. I'm tellin' you, there ain't no one else here besides me and you."

"I feel like I'm losing my mind."

"Well, maybe it's all just a big misunderstanding."

"What do you mean?"

"The sound. Maybe it's just some kind of weird echo. An *acoustical anomaly.*"

"An *acoustical anomaly?*"

"Yeah, like the shape of the room is creating some kind of Doppler Effect or something, ya know?"

"No, I actually don't know. What the hell is the Doppler Effect?"

"It's like, uhmm, well, I suppose I don't quite know what it is either. It has something to do with sound though. Or maybe it was weather . . . "

"Jeezus Christ, Myles. I know what I heard. And it certainly wasn't the acoustics or the goddamn weather. They were fuckin' footsteps. As clear as day."

Elenya was on the verge of tears, getting all worked up, chest heaving in and out like she had fire in her lungs. And she'd just yelled at him. She never yelled at him. They weren't that kind of couple. They were still newlyweds. They still liked each other.

Plus, she was right. They *were* footsteps. And Myles knew it.

"Okay, okay. I heard it too, El. I'm confused as hell and freakin' the fuck out and I don't have any more idea about what's going on around here than you do, alright? We had a long day. I'm overworked. Overtired. And I got all sortsa emotions bubblin' up inside me. Call it a hunch, but I'd bet the farm you're feelin' the same. Moving sucks. I know I don't hafta tell you that. You were carrying those boxes right alongside me. Bet your feet are barkin' and your back is sore and you got a buncha fresh callouses on your palms, same as I do. We're in this together, Ellie Beans. And although I want answers just as much as you do, I think maybe we should try an' save whatever little sleep we can an' look into this again in the morning. Just a few more winks. That's all I'm sayin'. Give us a chance to reapproach this problem with some fresh eyes. I'm exhausted. I need it. *We* need it. A good night's sleep an' then I promise you, we can spend the whole afternoon on the Mystery of the Invisible Tap Dancer, or whatever the hell we're dealin' with here. Once sober minds prevail, I'm ab-so-fuh-king-lute-ly sure we'll find a perfectly rational explanation for everything we've just seen and heard, yeah?"

Elenya furrowed her brow and chewed the inside of her cheek. Myles paid her no heed. He wrapped his arms around her shoulders, folded her into himself, and gave her a tender peck on the top of the head. She leaned into his broad body, cheek to chest. Safe in his embrace. This was his magic trick. When he turned on the 'big strong man' schtick, he could still melt her like butter, and though she found his tone somewhat condescending, at least in this case, he actually made a valid point. Perhaps some more sleep would do her good. Perhaps she was making a big deal out of nothing. She was so goddamn tired that she felt like she was going to collapse.

The silence had returned. Wonderful silence. *Restful* silence. Elenya let her husband lead her back to the bedroom, and this time, the only footsteps they could hear were their own.

DAY ONE

THIS
IS
OUR
SKY

II

DAYBREAK **CREPT FROM** the east, one block at a time, washing over the city until it arrived on their doorstep. Heaven above them transitioned from black to blue, the sky like a freshly formed bruise.

Elenya never fell back asleep. Neither did Myles. Eyes open, bodies still, they lay together in the darkness, silently waiting for the dawn to arrive.

And now the night was over and yesterday lingered like a half-remembered dream, details faded and conflated, already a miasma of plot points, like a fairy tale they'd been told a long time ago. Like their lives before that morning belonged to somebody else.

Day one in the new place, and there was still so much work to do. Aside from their fancy new mattress and a few bathroom provisions, they hadn't even begun to unpack. Cardboard boxes filled the apartment, stacked up in towers, hastily labeled in permanent black marker. STATIONERY and TOWELS and ASSORTED KITCHEN STUFF. Clothing stuffed into garbage bags for easy transport. Dishes wrapped in newspaper.

The entire afternoon prior was spent carrying all their possessions inside. From the back of the U-Haul to the living room. Back and forth, back and forth, back and forth they scuttled, like two little ants trying to build an anthill.

"Where should I put this?" Myles asked as he walked through the wide-open front door carrying two boxes balanced on top of each other, both marked COFFEE MUGS.

"Anywhere for now," Elenya replied. "Along the wall? Over by the couch? Doesn't matter. We'll organize it all tomorrow an' figure out where this stuff goes."

That was the plan, anyway. But then, in the morning:

13

"Myles! Myles, come in here! Quick!" Elenya shouted as she stepped into the living room.

Her husband hustled in behind her, bathrobe untied, bare chest and boxers exposed. This was the least of his concerns, of course. Myles gasped as well.

The mold grew on everything.

E-V-E-R-Y-T-H-I-N-G.

Almost like it came out of nowhere. There was nothing to note only a few short hours ago. Now the whole goddamn apartment was coated in it. A sour sheen, glistening and foul. The smell was like swamp water. Like fermented vegetation. A stagnant death scent. Elenya covered her mouth to keep from getting sick.

"Sweet Baby Jeezus, what the fuck happened?!?" Myles cried out, his chin tucked into his neck, trying to hold his breath, the stench so powerful he could feel it bypassing his nostrils and permeating his skin.

"Myles?"

"Yeah?"

"I think we might have a bit of a mold problem."

"Yeah."

Her eyes darted around the room to the ribbons of mildew streaked like claw marks across their formerly white walls. Nothing a little soap and water couldn't fix, she figured, but still, from the baseboards to the ceiling, nothing was spared. It even started to creep up the arm of the threadbare couch. She could see the stuffing where the fabric had been eaten thin.

"How the hell did it spread so fast?"

"I don't know."

"Does it normally grow this fast?"

"I have no idea, Ellie. I'm not a fuckin' *mold doctor* or whatever the hell they're called. Maybe it happened when we opened the cabinets under the kitchen sink?"

"And now it's all over the living room?"

"Yeah, I guess."

"I think this is something else, Myles. Look."

Oblong patches of cadaver-gray mold sprung forth from the floorboards, from the front door to the hallway before doubling back and zigzagging about. This mysterious mycelium encircled the newlyweds like they'd been cordoned off. The living room was a minefield of gossamer fuzz.

"What do those patches look like to you, huh?"

Myles bit his lip like he was trying to pin it shut.

"Footsteps," he replied, voice awarble, barely above a whisper, as if acknowledging the problem somehow made it more real. "They look like footprints."

Elenya gave her husband an anxious look as if to ask him, *what the hell is going on here, Myles?* And Myles returned her gaze with an equally demure expression.

I don't know, his eyes seemed to reply.

And then a silhouette of a man suddenly appeared in their front window, his exaggerated shadow cast like Nosferatu across their floor.

The newlyweds instinctively ducked behind one of the cardboard towers, doing their damnedest to not touch the mold and stay out of sight.

Elenya tracked the figure like a jet-lagged panther while Myles scanned the room. He picked up the book they'd left sitting on top of the coffee table—the one they'd both been intending to read, but just couldn't find the time—and wielded it like a weapon. A hardcover copy of *Don Quixote* by Miguel de Cervantes. Not quite as effective as a sword and shield, but it was thick enough to do some damage should the need arise.

"Who is that?" she asked.

"I can't tell."

"What do they want?"

"How should I know?"

"So why are we hiding then?"

Myles looked at the book in his hands like he didn't know how it got there.

"That's a good question," he said.

"Hello?" the man outside the window called out. "Anybody home? Ding dong! Avon Calling! You just won the Publisher's Clearing House sweepstakes. Do you have a moment to talk about our Lord and Savior, Jesus Christ?"

Myles leaned out from behind the box. Squinted against the light.

"Wait . . . is that . . . the dude from next door?" he asked.

Elenya leaned out from the other side and squinted too.

"I think so?" she said. "Landlord said his name was Brad. I think he runs the Neighborhood Watch or something."

"The Neighborhood Watch?" scoffed Myles as he stood up and finally tied shut his bathrobe. He greeted his neighbor with a single, congenial wave.

"Peekaboo! I see-eeeee you!" Brad nearly sung as he spoke, a big dumb smile plastered across his puffy face, pressed up against the glass, hands cupped over his eyes like a visor to block out the sun. A greasy comb-over crested the top of his potato-shaped head, making him look like Peter Lorre in those old Bugs Bunny cartoons. Pills of sweat sat on his brow like his hairline was weeping.

"Brad, I presume?" said Myles.

"Guilty as charged," Brad replied.

"You make a habit of looking in people's windows like that, Brad?"

"Huh? Oh, no, no, you're a special case. Hah. I'm kidding. Actually, I wanted to come by and introduce myself. Say hello. I live in the apartment to the right of you. Unit 7." He took a step back, lit a cigarette, and exhaled. His affable visage was lost amid the smog. "I saw y'all unloading your stuff yesterday. Woulda offered to help, of course, but I threw my back out last weekend doin' a couple of repairs round the ole homestead. You know how it is. We're gettin' older every day."

There was definitely something off about this man, thought Myles, though he couldn't quite put his finger on what exactly it was. He was almost *too* friendly. *Too* animated. *Too* verbose. His mannerisms had a rehearsed quality to them, like he was a stage performer or carnival barker putting on a show.

"Hey Brad, can I ask you a quick question?"

"Sure. Anything you need, bud. I'm an open book."

"Actually, there's no reason for us to keep shouting through this glass. I'mma come outside, hold on just a sec."

Myles turned the handle, but the door wouldn't open.

He double-checked the locks. Tried it again. And again, it didn't budge.

Maybe the wood is warped, he thought before realizing the whole thing was made out of aluminum. *Okay, so maybe the* aluminum *is warped then,* he said to himself. Though, obviously, he knew that wasn't the case.

Foot against the wall for leverage, he twisted the knob, pulling with all his might. Tapeworm-thick veins crawled across his forehead. Grunting. Straining. Myles turned beet red. Yet, in the end, he found no purchase. Not even the click of the deadbolt rattling around in the latch. Something inside it was gumming up the works.

He leaned in and noticed the mold caked into the cracks. Somehow it had spread to there too, filling up the space along the length of the frame. As thick as putty. As durable as cement.

One last jerk of the handle, though he knew it was futile. They were sealed in from the inside. At least for the time being.

"You okay in there?" the muffled voice of Brad came through the door.

"What's wrong?" Elenya asked her husband.

"It's stuck."

"What do you mean it's stuck?"

"I mean exactly what I'm saying, Ellie. It's full of mold, pretty much running the entire length of the jamb. It's like glue or something. I can't get it open."

"Problem?" said Brad as he peered back in through the window.

"The mold . . . " but before Myles could finish his sentence, Brad dismissed him with a wave of the hand.

"Having a bit of an issue, I take it?" he said.

"The door won't open."

"Yeah, I can see that," said Brad. "And have you tried the windows yet?"

"The windows?"

Brad nodded to the sill.

Mucus green slime caulked the crevices, gray fuzz resting on top like the stubble on an old man's chin. It grew out of the cracks and across the vinyl frame. Even the glass itself had taken on a frosty quality as a light layer of mold attached itself to the facade. Myles hadn't noticed it before, but now that he did, it was indisputable. The window was sealed, same as the front door.

Myles grabbed the stile and tried to pry it open, palms pawing the glass. Elenya joined in, too. The DeNovas worked together, white knuckled, pushing upward with their collective might. Still, no dice. The whole thing might as well have been cast in stone.

An unfazed Brad silently watched from the opposite side as the panicked couple quickly lost steam and eventually gave up.

"Can you check the one in the bedroom, too?" Myles asked his wife. And off Elenya ran. He could hear her banging around the other side of the apartment, grunting as she tried to yank the bedroom window open. A minute later, she returned, shaking her head. Nope. Nada. Not even a smidgen. It, too, was sealed tight.

Brad took a final drag of his cigarette, dropped the butt, and stomped it out. Factory-thick plumes of smoke rose from his nostrils.

"Damn. That really sucks, you guys. But you know how these old buildings are, don'tcha? A leaky pipe, a drippy drain, whatever the case may be—it don't take much. Just the tiniest bit of moisture in the walls and *boom*! Mildew. Mold. Dry rot. You name it. Clawing its way outta every nook and cranny."

"Is this a common problem?" asked Elenya.

"It can be," replied Brad.

"Aren't they supposed to disclose these kindsa things before we move in?" a flustered Myles said. He was grinding his teeth and his fists were clenched into ineffectual balls.

Good-natured Brad simply shook his head. Newlyweds, he thought. So oblivious. So charmingly sincere.

"Look, you guys're gonna be fine. I've lived here for years and I'm doing okay. I cleaned myself up, and you can do it too. This mold issue you're talkin' about? This ain't nothin'. It's justa flat tire, in the grand scheme of things. It'sa pair of wet socks. Take a quick look over my shoulder. Whaddaya see? Justa same ole city it's always been. And the world ain't any different this mornin' than it was last night. Ya know, this whole situation reminds me of a news article I read the other day about some kid in Haiti who was born with his skin turned inside out. Just flipped right around. A one-in-a-billion chance. All his nerve endings were sticking out, exposed to the elements. He was in constant agony, the doctors said. He lived to be nearly ten and never had a second of joy. All I'm sayin' is you both got it better than a lotta people out there, that's f'sure."

"I'm sorry, Brad, but what the fuck are you even talkin' about?" Elenya barked, not so much a question as it was a demand.

Brad glared at her, smile instantly dropping. Somehow his eyes appeared darker than they had a moment before. Like two little raisins lodged into his skull.

"What I'm sayin', *Ellie*, is that your skin ain't on inside out, so perhaps you should take a deep breath and chill the fuck out. Things ain't so bad. Do you understand?"

He held his raisin-eyed gaze on them.

The newlyweds exchanged a nervous glance.

No, Brad. They didn't understand.

The DeNovas didn't understand at all.

III

Hot **COFFEE.** Even through the mildew they could smell it, invigorating and familiar. Two mugs were filled to the brim with tire-black liquid, and wisps of steam like calligraphy curled through the air. The taste was bitter on their tongues, but they needed the jolt. The blacker, the better, the DeNovas always said. The ends justified the means. Function over form.

Perhaps Brad was right. Perhaps it was unrealistic to assume everything would always be perfect all the time. Elenya and Myles had their whole lives ahead of them. They had a roof over their heads. They had each other. They were *privileged* to be in this position in the first place. Some people were born without any arms or legs. Once they cleaned up the apartment and filed everything away, they could put this whole ghastly first day behind them. They could start planning their next step. And the one after that.

Myles sprayed the footprint-shaped spots on the floor with Clorox, letting the bleach bubble up, frizzle and fry. Fuzzy gray fibers recoiled in its caustic wake. Then a quick wipe from the paper towel and it was as good as new.

Elenya made her way through the boxes, deconstructing the towers from the top down. Fungus spread across the bottom edge of each cardboard tower. It looked like necrotic flesh turning to rot on the bone.

The boxes weren't stacked in any logical order, and the fact that she had to stop and inspect every item inside for mold made for slow work. Most things were salvageable so long as she took the time to wipe them down. This was a delicate kind of surgery. Q-tips and cotton balls. Multiple rolls of paper towels. The garbage was piling up quickly, not to mention the fumes. The apartment remained hermetically sealed along all the exit points, though Myles was determined to resolve that today.

After he finished with the footprints, he moved onto the door. Squirt. Squirt. *Sizzle*. Wipe.

"Hmm . . ."

"What's up?" Elenya called out from the kitchen. She was in the middle of organizing their dry goods. Soup, noodles, and other non-perishables—all stacked up in the cupboard. She duct-taped the cabinet under the sink closed, hopefully interring the strange growth inside.

She joined her husband in the living room and placed a hand on his shoulder. The two of them faced the front door together.

"Watch," he said as he once again pulled the trigger on his bottle of bleach. The astringent solution filled up the jamb like acid rain. Like the biblical flood. The mold sizzled so loudly it sounded like a scream, though perhaps it was not the death rattle the DeNovas were hoping for. Pustules appeared and erupted like a string of viscous pearls and some kind of pinkish-reddish syrup oozed forth, not quite blood, but of similar composition. This hideous new discharge cut through the melt like a salve, instantly "healing" the door over behind it. A fresh strip of cottony fuzz formed along the frame like a raised scar.

"It's growing faster than I can dissolve it."

"Have you tried the windows yet? Maybe we'd have better luck there?"

Myles slid over and gave the window the same treatment. Squirt. Wipe. Squirt. Wipe. Squirt. Wipe. Several times over. The mold blistered. Crusted over. Dug itself deeper into the sill.

"Jeezus."

"It looks worse than when I started," he said.

"It *smells* worse than it did, too," Elenya concurred.

"It smells like shit."

"Like dead shit."

"Left to canker in the sun."

"I can't believe how cavalier that dude next door is acting about all of this," she said. "You heard the way he was talking. Like we were the weird ones for bringing it up."

"I'm guessing maybe the mold ain't as bad in his apartment?"

"You think the landlord knows?"

"How could he not?" Myles ran an exasperated hand through his hair. "But just in case, I'mma shoot him an email tomorrow and let him know what's goin' on. Truth be told, he kinda struck me as the absentee type, but I'm thinkin' that once we get the door open I can run out to the Home Depot and buy us a dehumidifier or something. I'll send him a picture of the receipt an' see if we can get him to cover the expense. I mean, it's not like this is the first building in history to ever have mold in it, ya know? Figure there's gotta be protocols or legal precedents for this type'a thing."

"But don't you think *someone* shoulda said *something* to us about this before we signed the lease?"

"What would you want them to do, El? Put a neon sign above the door? HOUSE OF ROT in glowing pink letters like it was the entrance to a brothel?"

She gave him a playful shove. "Shut up. That's not what I meant."

"Be honest, would you have followed up on a Craigslist ad for a 'charming, mid-century 595 sq. ft. bungalow full of strange midnight noises and an alarmingly-resilient fungus, downtown adjacent, just minutes from public transit, only $1350 a month?'"

Now she laughed for real. "Okay, okay. Point taken. But still, we're the ones getting the short end of the stick here. I mean, what are those fucking footsteps about anyway? We got ghosts in here, too?"

"I don't believe in ghosts, Ellie."

"Neither do I, but we're sitting on ample evidence to the contrary."

He took his wife's slender hands into his. The two of them looked out the frosted window—their limited porthole to the outside world. A few feet of yellow grass separated their front stoop from the sidewalk, and beyond that, the city went about its business, the same as it always had, both unaware and uninterested in what was transpiring behind the featureless walls of this anonymous apartment. He gave her a peck on the top of the head. *Mwah.* Small but affectionate.

"It's gonna be alright, babe. We just gotta hang in there. I know this ain't the ideal situation, but let's try'ta focus on the positives, if we can. We're here and we're together. That's the most important thing. And barring a few of these UNFORESEEN

COMPLICATIONS, this apartment *is* exactly the kind of place we were looking for. Convenient. Inconspicuous. And most importantly, affordable."

Affordable. Yeah. That was the clincher.

Elenya recalled the first and only time they toured the place. The landlord took them through the unit, pointing out all the appliances, flipping switches off and on, pausing to let the newlyweds *ohhh* and *ahhh* at each one, like having electricity or a working stovetop was some kind of unparalleled luxury.

"This knob makes the water come out HOT and this knob makes it come out COLD," he said as he illustrated to them how the bathroom sink worked. "That's TWO temperatures for the price of ONE!"

And now look at them, all moved in, with their fancy hot water and fancy indoor plumbing. They were living like the Kardashians over here!

"Maybe we made a mistake," Elenya said to Myles, looking wistfully through the mold-sealed window. The red flags were there from the get-go, yet they actively chose to ignore them. "Maybe we shoulda moved into one of those high-rises they keep putting up all around town. Condo living ain't so bad. They're clean and safe. Some of 'em even have concierges."

"I don't care about a concierge."

"I know. I don't either."

"I hate those stupid fuckin' buildings. They got no personality to 'em."

"No history to 'em either."

"Though I actually looked at some of the listings when we first started browsing. The cheapest one I could find was half the size of this place and twice the price."

"Yeah, but it probably isn't rotting apart from the inside-out."

"Meh. Give it time."

More and more high-rises were being built every day. Or at least that was how it seemed. Big boxy structures, dozens of stories tall, all concrete and steel, flanking their rundown little apartment on all sides. "Warehouse chic" was how the real estate agents liked to describe them. "Yuppie prisons" was the term Elenya clapped back with, though not without the *slightest* twinge of jealousy in her voice. Overpriced and full of useless amenities, like free artisan coffee in the lobbies or discounted memberships to the local gym. Neighborhood after neighborhood, the city was razed and rebuilt on top of the still-twitching corpse of the past. Industrialized. Homogenized. Nearly identical in their slate-gray design. Gentrification spread outward from downtown like a pox.

But that was how it was. That was how it'd always been. That was progress, And progress was unstoppable. Rent prices were increasing. Wages were stagnating. Insurance premiums were going up while coverage was going down. The glamor of city life was perhaps not as glamorous as it initially seemed.

But the DeNovas worked hard for the things they wanted. The DeNovas were going to play it smart. The DeNovas had big plans, just you wait and see. This was all temporary, Elenya would remind herself, as if it were an incantation. At some point, we'll have this all figured out. We'll get better jobs. We'll find ourselves a house. We'll have a good life. A *normal* life. Like their parents had. Like they'd seen in the movies. The city wasn't their end goal. It was their starting point. Elenya always wanted to be a mother. Myles always wanted to be a dad. They would have kids someday when things were more stable. They would get a place out in the burbs, somewhere with a yard and garage and a pool in the back. Somewhere not too far away. Somewhere with a little less crime, a little less squalor. Somewhere near the city without being trapped inside of it. The plan was, live in a cheap apartment for now so they could put in a down payment somewhere else later. Fifteen miles or so down the interstate would be nice. Just a zipcode or two away. A place where things were calmer and quieter and not so *relentless.*

On their first date, Myles took Elenya to one of the many scenic overlooks hidden within the hills of the westernmost tip of town. His shitty old Honda Civic zoomed up the twisted and moss-lined roads, beyond what you'd find in any of the travelogues or tourist guides, to a public patch of grass and a few scattered park benches tucked away on the side of a mountain, high above the city.

The trees here were cleared so their view was unobstructed. They had a bottle of wine and a blanket in the backseat. A Bluetooth speaker so they could play a couple tunes. They were going to have a picnic, just the two of them at the top of the world.

Downtown opened before them like a pop-up book. Miles upon

miles, until it disappeared into the horizon. The true size and scale of the landscape, equal parts humbling and grand.

Their love back then was nascent. A caterpillar in a cocoon, a creature as yet unformed. They barely knew each other. But there was something special about this boy, thought Elenya. And likewise, there was something special about her, Myles agreed. Maybe they didn't quite understand it yet, but they could undoubtedly *feel* it. Something was happening there. Some unstoppable process had already begun. They had no choice but to lean into it. To let go. To fall in love and let it take them where it may.

They drank the wine and got tipsy and flirted and laughed, and Myles climbed up on the old stone wall that marked the overlook's edge. There was a sharp precipice on the other side, dangerous and sheer. If he were to lose his footing, he'd fall a couple of hundred feet to his fatal end before rolling down the mountainside a couple of hundred more. He helped Elenya up so she was standing there next to him. The city was like a postcard, glossy and unsoiled.

"One day, all of this will be ours," he said, arms stretched wide as if he was performing some kind of magic trick only she could see.

Elenya adopted the pose. She held her arms out too. Kept her eyes forward. Focused on the city in front of them and not the drop underfoot. From their point of view, it almost appeared as if they were flying.

"We're like birds!" she said, refusing to look down. When they joined hands and stood side by side, their wingspan encompassed the entire horizon.

Myles nodded in agreement. "This is our sky."

That was a good day. And they'd had a lot of good days since. And even though they were now trapped in this strange new apartment—with mold like television static creeping in from the edges of the window frame, the city shrunk to the size of a rectangle, offering them only a stagnant view—they still faithfully, and perhaps foolishly, held out hope for the future. Their home was but a hovel, a tiny refuge nested within the belly of an organism much more complicated than they'd ever understand. From this window, they could see only a small stretch of street. A few squares of sidewalk. The concrete building across the way. It looked like nothing and everything at the same time.

Elenya sighed, resting her head against her husband's shoulder.

"I'll keep working on this," he said, motioning to the door jamb. "Maybe I can try some of those other cleaners we got. I don't know. If the problem persists tomorrow, I'll give the landlord a call and have him send a professional out. And if he doesn't answer or refuses to help, I'll call the fire marshal or the Better Business Bureau or whomever it is you report these kinds of things to. Hell, I'll even call a tenant lawyer and we'll sue his ass if we gotta. Point is, there's no need to worry, Ellie. I'mma get this fixed as soon as I can. Everything is gonna be alright."

IV

THE TINTINNABULATION OF a muffled piano filled the apartment with music, a set of skilled fingers dancing up and down the ivories, passionate and professional. It was a recording of *Für Elise* by Ludwig van Beethoven, the volume turned up so high you could hear the white noise of the auditorium roaring between the scales. Myles and Elenya stopped what they were doing and faced the wall, confused.

"What the hell?" said Myles.

"Guess that dude next door is into the classics?"

"It'sa bit loud, don'tcha think?"

"Yeah. Though it kinda sounds like the wall is amplifying it somehow. I don't know if that makes sense or not. Come put your hand against it. Do you feel the vibrations?"

Myles joined Elenya and pressed his palm flat against the drywall, the palpitation of each successive note rippling through it like the heartbeat of a hidden giant.

Elenya closed her eyes, letting the concerto wash over her.

"Pretty song, though," she said.

Myles nodded in agreement. "Yeah. Makes me think about Doritos, though."

She turned to him, baffled. "Did you say Doritos?"

"Yeah. They're tortilla chips. They're fuckin' delicious."

"Jesus Christ, I know what Doritos are, Myles. I just don't know why the hell you're bringing them up."

"It was a commercial from a few years back. Don'tcha remember? We open on Ludwig van Beethoven at his piano amidst a crippling bout of writer's block, tapping out a few sour and discordant notes before slamming his fists down on the keyboard in frustration. 'Oont I'll never complete mein magnum opus' he says as he crumples up the page of sheet music he was working on, tossing it over his shoulder to join the others on the floor. All hope seems lost. But then the door to his chamber suddenly bursts open and in storms an attractive but stern-looking maid. Balanced on one hand is a silver serving platter, on top of which rests a bag of Cool Ranch Doritos. 'Vhat is zee meaning of zhis, Elise?' Beethoven asks as she thrusts it in his direction. 'You've been woorking too hard, Mr. Ludvig, oont you need to eat somezhing,' she replies. The maid raises a knowing eyebrow as Beethoven pulls a chip out of the bag and takes a bite. His face immediately lights up, struck by the spark of divine inspiration. He turns back to his piano where he not only instantly composes *Für Elise* in its entirety, but he is also so moved by this whole Dorito-induced experience that he can't help but spontaneously burst out into accompanying lyrics as well: '*My dear Elise/I am so pleased/Can you bring me/Some nacho cheese/And I must say/That I feel great/Doritos are/So taste-tayyy.*' The logo appears onscreen. DORITOS, it says, NOW IN POPPIN' JALAPEÑO AND SALSA VERDE FLAVORS. Then the ad break ends and we're back to watching reruns of *How I Met Your Mother.*"

" . . . uhhh, guess I musta missed that one," she said.

Myles shrugged. "Ah. Well, if I'm bein' honest, I don't think it was historically accurate anyway. I mean, Cool Ranch wasn't even introduced until 1986 so that's an anachronism right there."

The track ended. They could hear Brad shuffling around, switching the phonograph off. *Click.* The music disappeared as abruptly as it arrived, and the newlyweds got back to work.

Elenya unpacked the last of their belongings from the boxes. Sundries made their way to the medicine cabinet. Clothes were folded and placed in the dresser drawers. She pulled out a couple of framed photographs she intended to hang up. Their wedding day. Their first dance. A moment forever frozen in time. Myles in his tuxedo. Elenya in her white gown. Smiling. Laughing. That was a good day, she thought as she drove the nail into the gypsum, the thud of her hammer an entirely different kind of concerto as a droplet of congealed green goo streaked down from the hole. Elenya figured it must be some slime mold from between the walls. She spritzed the glob with bleach and hung the picture on top of it. Outta sight, outta mind.

HOUSE OF ROT

Myles resumed his assault on the front door. It was a painstaking process, very trial-and-error. He didn't know shit about remediation. Clorox. Windex. Ajax. Pine-Sol. Even a couple rounds of soap and water. You name it, he tried it. The mold would sizzle away and almost immediately return, repairing itself faster than he could destroy it. Scouring it proved useless. Drying it out didn't seem to work either. He heated up a butter knife on the gas range and jammed it into the crack between the door and the jamb to try and melt it away.

"Burn, motherfucker! Burn!" he said through clenched teeth, but instead, the hot steel had the opposite effect. The mold proliferated in the wake of the blade, oxidizing the metal so quickly Myles could hear it hiss. It browned. Corroded. Crumbled apart.

He tossed it into the already-unmanageable pile of garbage in the kitchen.

"Myles, that knife was part of a set."

"I'll buy us a new one."

Elenya finished placing her books on the shelf. Sliding a copy of *Galapagos* by Kurt Vonnegut Jr. between *A Short History of Nearly Everything* by Bill Bryson and *I Miss the World* by Violet LeVoit. The shelves were not arranged in alphabetical order, as one might expect, but rather through a clandestine system of her own design. Myles never quite understood it.

She stood back and admired her handiwork. The rainbow of spines. Tens of thousands of pages. Everything except *Don Quixote*, which still sat on the coffee table behind her. She swore she'd get to it one of these days. Once things were calmer. Once they were all settled in.

Myles continued to run circles. Vacuum cleaner out, tube pressed against the crack, teeth grinding, nostrils flared, maniacal expression on his face like *suck on this, ya bastard! Whirrrrrrrr.* But he was still no closer to finishing than when he started.

"Hey, Myles?" Elenya laid a delicate hand on his hunched shoulder. "Mye?"

He switched the vacuum off, wincing as he stood up straight. His back had cramped and he hadn't even noticed. He felt beat up. Like he'd been tenderized.

"Argh. Ouch. Spasm or something."

"Why don't you put that thing away and call it quits for now, babe?"

"I'm not done, Ellie."

"I know, but it'll still be there in the morning, won't it?"

"Yeah. It will be. That's exactly the problem."

"Look, we've been busting our asses all day tryin' to get this place in order. And all things considered, we're almost done. It's just gonna take a little more elbow grease than we initially thought."

"Elbow grease?"

"It ain't nothing you and I can't handle."

"I just wanna get settled."

"I know you do. And I want that too. But these things take as long as they take, ya know? Everything is a process. One step at a time. Rome wasn't built in a day."

"No, I suppose it wasn't," he said. "But didn't it burn down overnight while that Nero dude sat around playing with his fiddle?"

The soft smile on her face was like a port in the storm. Myles let her lead him over to the couch, where he plopped down so hard it sent a cloud of dust out of the cushions.

Elenya was right. The sun had set an hour ago. He was beyond tired. His brain was frazzled and his body was sore. He wasn't equipped to deal with this shit. He hadn't the tools, nor the knowledge, nor—apparently—the stamina. Tomorrow morning he would make the appropriate calls. He would get a professional to come out. Someone who knew what they were doing. A specialist. A hazmat crew. Whoever it took. Let it be their problem. Let them fix it. He had enough on his plate. He had TOO MUCH on his plate. His plate runneth over like he was at the goddamn buffet.

V

THE FIRST DAY in their new apartment was winding down. The DeNovas ate dinner together at the small table in the kitchen amid the piles of trash. Peanut butter and jelly sandwiches with a pickle on the side. Low effort. No frills. Filling and familiar.

They caught up on their favorite TV shows on Netflix and Prime, feet touching as they sat at opposite ends of the sofa. They discussed all the as-yet unresolved plot threads. They speculated on how each series would end, talking about these fictional people as if they were real people. As if they were old friends they used to have. As if their exploits were a part of the old lives they used to live. They were married now. They had a lot more responsibilities these days. They were settling down. They were building a life together. Newer adventures awaited them still. They were between seasons, is all.

Elenya and Myles climbed into bed where they made efficient yet tender love under the thick, down comforter. Myles knew how to touch her. Elenya knew how to respond. They had good sex. They always had good sex, even if it was a tad uneventful.

And the night grew longer.

And they eventually went to sleep.

And all was silent.

And then the footsteps returned.

They echoed even louder than they had the night before, so loud it was as if they'd multiplied in their absence. Instead of one set of feet, it sounded like dozens. Elenya's eyes shot open.

"Not again," Elenya muttered to herself. They'd already established it was an *acoustical anomaly*, had they not? She figured her mind must have been playing tricks on her.

The footsteps stomped around the apartment. Rattling

doorknobs. Shuffling through items. Slamming kitchen drawers. It was a cacophony.

Elenya lay motionless, blanket pulled up to her chin. Fear flowed through her like her own blood. She didn't believe in ghosts, she reminded herself.

Myles slept under the sheets next to her, and the dull heat of his body wafted her way. She touched his leg with her big toe. He was such a solid sleeper. With this fancy new mattress, he might not wake up at all.

More footsteps. Pitter-patter. She tried to picture it in her head as a just storm cloud passing. Hail pounding against the roof. Wind rattling the windows. Thunder rumbling through her bones. Just a temporary situation. Nothing to get worked up about.

Up the hall and back down again, invisible feet filled the darkness, coming at her in waves. Lapping against all her shores. There was an unexpected rhythm to it, like a marching band. Or soldiers on patrol. Or construction workers stomping around as they put up another high-rise in the lot next door.

That must be it, she figured. Another high-rise going up. Undoubtedly identical to the one across the street. The construction crews were closing in. Circling the DeNovas like sharks. Elenya knew that one day too this apartment would be nothing but rubble. But she figured her and Myles would be long gone by then. Right?

In her mind's eye, Elenya could see the foreman of this invisible construction crew standing in her living room, clipboard in his hands. He was going through all her belongings. Marking things down. Taking notes. He held her entire life under scrutiny. He was the auditor. He alone determined what was worth saving and what was junk.

The foreman slowly made his way through the rest of the apartment. Eventually entering the bedroom. Step by heavy step. To Elenya, everything felt underwaterish, like in a dream. She was too terrified to even move.

And there he was. In her room, in front of her. His features were obscured. His intentions were oblique. He was like a chalk outline at some kind of old crime scene, barely visible as he loomed above. A man without a face. And yet there was something familiar about him—and about this whole situation—she couldn't quite put her finger on. It was like she'd been there before, though it was not quite déjà vu as Elenya had ever experienced it in the past. This was something far more innate and harder to explain. A knowledge that this moment was and had been and always would be, and that there was no version of reality in which it would or could ever be altered.

So sorry to wake you. The foreman spoke to Elenya though he had no mouth. His words were not words. His voice was not a voice. His missives appeared in her head as if they were her own thoughts. *Another day or two,* he said. *We'll be done here soon.*

What are you building? she said to him in the same unlanguage, using the same untongue. Her voice was nothing more than a vestigial organ. This was an impossible conversation with an impossible conversationalist. It didn't feel real.

We're building a castle, he replied.

A castle?

Indeed.

With spires?

Oh yes.

And a drawbridge?

Of course.

Like in the fairy tales?

Exactly. Just like in all those storybooks you used to read when you were a kid, once upon a time, they always started, though perhaps not so far away now.

I've always wanted to live in a castle.

It is for you.

For me?

And Myles too. This is your castle. Or it will be, once the work is complete.

You're building me a castle?

Yes.

I don't understand.

But you said it yourself. It's what you've always wanted.

But why? Why me? Why us? What have we done to deserve it?

What have you done to deserve it? He repeated her question as if he were weighing it on a scale. *What have you done that makes you think you don't?*

"What would you want them to do, El? Put a neon sign above the door? HOUSE OF ROT in glowing letters like it was the entrance to a brothel?"

DAY TWO

LIKE
A
SCAR
THAT
REFUSED
TO
HEAL

VI

"**F**UCK."

"Fuck fuckity fuck fuck fuck."

Myles grasped for a cogent thought but found only a series of expletives instead, strung together in his mind like rosary beads. The motherfucking mold problem was so much fucking worse this morning than it was the fucking day before.

Two distinct sets of footprints cut a corrosive path through the living room—a waltz of destruction now blossomed in an array of fungi so thick it almost looked like a carpet—inside of which all sorts of new colors were born, as the grays and greens gave way to pinks and reds and blacks. Fleshy and swollen and gooey all at once, like a festering wound on the floor itself. Like a scar that refused to heal.

"Ellie, come in here. And bring the peroxide."

The mold was concentrated toward the center of the room before branching out—a nexus point where the boxes were piled up yesterday afternoon. Pungent as it chewed through the stale apartment air, smelling both earthy, like mildew, and coppery, like blood. Elenya entered behind her husband, a bottle of peroxide in hand. She stopped short, eyes wide, almost gagging as she hit the stink.

"Fuck fuckity fuck."

"My sentiments exactly."

Slime bubbled forth from the thicker patches like a wave of psychedelic sea foam. Defying gravity as it blistered up the walls. It entrenched itself deeper into the couch cushions, excreting a coil of black gunk behind it like fish shit. The legs of the coffee table looked like meaty-mottled bones. A supernovae-shaped bloom spread out from behind their wedding picture. Tiny hyphae rose from the mold, a miniature mushroom forest, stalks almost as thick as the unshaven hair on Myles' chin. Some kind of hideous evolution was taking place in this apartment, and in the span of a night, it had quickly advanced beyond their control.

Myles took a deep breath, trying to keep calm. Elenya slipped a reassuring hand into his, though she too was on the verge of hyperventilating. Both their palms were clammy and cold. She could hear the phlegm rattling around in her husband's chest.

"You feelin' okay?" she asked him. She noticed a couple extra wrinkles pinching the corners of his bloodshot eyes. He appeared gaunter than usual. Skin looked waxy too. His complexion gone wan.

"No, I'm not *feeling okay*. Take a look around, Ellie. Nothing about this is okay. Nothing about this makes any sense."

Elenya felt the phlegm knocking around in her chest as well. The oppressive weight of exhaustion cast a dim light on her normally glowing features. Dark bags formed under her sunken eyes. Joints achy. Muscles sore. Lips so dry you could see the ridges on them, and her nose was red and raw and running like a leaky spigot. *Sniffle sniffle snort.* Like she was trying to keep her brains from leaking out.

"What is happening to us?" she said.

"It's gotta be the *eggs*. We're breathing 'em all in. It's making us sick."

"Eggs?"

"Or whatever they're called. I don't know the names of stuff. I work in a call center, fer god's sake. They don't even like us to go off-script. You know what I mean though, like how it shoots 'em out when it's tryin' to reproduce." Myles wiggled his fingers to simulate a cloud of moldy dust raining down around her.

"Are you talking about *spores*?"

"Yeah. Spores. That's it. We're breathin' in the spores. Didja know I'm allergic to penicillin? It's true. Makes me break out in hives. And look at my arm. Hives!"

"The footsteps came back last night. Even louder than they were the day before. I was half-asleep. I can't explain what I saw. Figured it musta been a bad dream." Her gaze drifted to the mold streaked across their floor like bloody trails through the slushy snow. "Though it seems like this nightmare ain't content to stay in my head."

"These are our prints, Ellie."

"What?"

"The footprints. They're our feet. These tracks belong to us."

He placed his right foot next to one of the right-foot-shaped patches. The curve of the arch. The size and shape of the sole. Toes like fugitives standing in a police lineup. There was no mistaking what they were looking at. It was an exact match.

"What the fuck?"

"We must've unwittingly spread it around yesterday when we were setting up the apartment. The moisture from our bodies acting like a catalyst or something? Look at 'em, Ellie. It's just us. Running in circles."

Myles took the bottle of peroxide. He popped the top and gave it a squirt. The faintest of sizzles could be heard, muted beneath the fuzz, almost like mocking laughter rising from below. Unsurprisingly, the antiseptic was completely ineffective against the moldering expanse. Myles hadn't the tools nor the skillset to handle this kind of problem. He hadn't the tools nor the skillset to handle MOST problems. They certainly didn't teach you how to deal with this kind of stuff in school, and even if they did, he never paid much attention, anyway.

He snapped the top shut and tossed the bottle away.

"Guess it's time we called someone, eh?"

VII

THEY **PLODDED BACK** to the bedroom. Myles grabbed his phone off the nightstand and swiped a finger across the screen, but it wouldn't turn on.

"Shit. It's dead. You got yours on you?"

Elenya pulled her phone out of her bathrobe pocket, unlocked it, and handed it to her husband. He gave the keypad a tap. A confused look crossed his face. Tap. Tap tap tap. Tapping the screen over and over again as if his thumbs were defibrillators.

"The hell?"

"Huh?"

"What's wrong with this stupid thing?"

"What do you mean?"

"It's all glitched out or something."

"Lemme see . . . "

Elenya took the phone and gave it a tap as well. Pixels filled the display like digital confetti, blinking on and off. Non-responsive. Hot to the touch, and getting hotter still.

"What happened to it?"

"How the hell should I know?"

"I don't know. It's your fucking phone."

"Don't yell at me, Myles."

"I'm not yelling. I'm . . . talking loudly."

"What's the difference?"

"Look—did you try turning it off and turning it back on again?" She attempted to cycle the power.

"It's not working. The buttons don't do anything."

"Maybe a factory reset?"

"Myles, I just told you, it's not working."

HOUSE OF ROT

And then it shorted out completely. *Zzst*. Now a brick in her hand.

"Maybe the smoke is a *good* thing?" Myles naively said.

She flipped the phone over and popped open the back. Cobweb-like strips of mold were growing inside it, mushroom-capped tendrils choking out the circuitry, so thick it almost looked like plant bark.

Myles popped open the back of his phone as well. It was also full of mold, the battery corroded and cracked, lithium leaking out of the side in a font of caustic white foam.

"Jeezus, Myles. Now what do we do?"

"What about the wifi? You have your computer nearby?"

Elenya flipped open her laptop. Checked the connection. "Internet is down. I think this shit musta got in the modem too."

"Hmm. Alright. Follow me. C'mon."

He barreled back into the living room, Elenya trailing a half-step behind.

"What are you doing?" she asked as Myles once again picked the hefty hardcover copy of *Don Quixote* up off the coffee table.

He opened it up and thumbed through the pages, thinking to himself that one day, he'd read this fucking book. One day. One day. Just not today.

"The fool knows more in his own house than the wise man in someone else's." he read the quick passage aloud to his wife. And then he launched it as hard as he could at the window.

Donk.

It struck the glass and bounced right off, windmilling backward through the air before hitting the floor with a thud. Mildew and mold instantly splattered across the cover, the Man of La Mancha now adrift in a sea of rot.

Of course this wasn't going to work, Myles thought. Nothing was working this morning. Nothing felt like it would ever work again.

But they still had to try. Both Myles and Elenya knew that was all they could do. Get something heavier. Throw it harder. Beat their fists against the wall until the room collapsed around them.

Elenya went to the kitchen, rifled through the pantry, and grabbed as many cans as she could carry. Split pea soup and refried beans. Budget dinners to accompany their budgeted lifestyle. They took turns pitching the non-perishables at the glass.

Donk. Donk. Donk. Donk.

But it was no use. They needed something heavier still.

Frustrated and covered in sweat, Myles peeled off his shirt in a virile—yet wholly unnecessary—display. For a moment, Elenya thought he was about to start beating his chest like a gorilla, though his once-muscular torso was now lean and covered in blotches, some so discolored and deep they looked as if they were about to cave in on themselves, his body a mineshaft on the verge of collapse.

He knotted the neck hole and the arms and turned his plain black tee into a makeshift sack, which he then filled with as many tin cans as he could fit. The fabric bulged but held—Pima cotton, it said along the neckline, woven strong and made to stretch— which it did as he lifted it above his head and swung it around like a medieval mace. Centrifugal force propelled him faster and faster with each rotation until it was a blur. It was a cannonball on a leash, explosive potential barely contained.

And he let it go.

And it hit the glass.

And it too bounced off—*Ka-BONG!*—and back into the room, striking Myles in the shoulder so hard he was knocked off his feet. He yelped as he hit the ground, pain so sharp and pervasive it felt like a swarm of tiny bees were trying to sting their way out of his body. Myles writhed amid the scattered soup cans and his now ripped shirt. And yet, the window remained uncracked. It might as well have been a sheet of titanium. It would take a demolitions expert to blast their way through.

Myles grumbled and massaged his shoulder until the joint popped back into place. The pain hadn't abated, but he could at least move his arm again.

Elenya gave the window a closer inspection, searching in vain for some kind of structural weakness, the single thread that could unravel the sweater, so to speak.

"Mye, come here. Look at this."

Myles struggled a moment but eventually stood and hobbled over. She motioned for him to lean in so he could see the layer of translucent mold lying in vein-like patterns across the windowpane, a lattice so fine and filamentous it appeared almost clear.

"Sweet Baby Jeezus, is the mold growing *inside* the glass?" Myles asked.

"Appears to be reinforcing it," Elenya replied.

"Maybe I'm not hitting it hard enough?"

"Yeah? And what does your shoulder hafta say about that?"

He was barely able to lift his arm, let alone swing that sack of soup cans around again.

"So what, then? We're stuck in here?" he said. "No phones? No way to communicate with the outside world? Not even a way to open the fuckin' door?"

"Someone is gonna notice we're gone, aren't they?"

"Eventually. Sure. But that could be days from now. Maybe even longer. They're not expecting me back at work until sometime next week."

"Next week?! What if something happens before then? What if there's a medical emergency? Or a fire? Myles, what if we're infected with this shit too? You saw what it did to our phones. Imagine what it could do to our bodies."

Myles ran a worried hand through his hair and when he pulled it back there were a couple of thick clumps stuck between his fingers. Stringy. Greasy. Pieces of scalp attached to the end. He touched his newly-formed bald spot, wincing as his finger found raw flesh, a dime-sized patch above his left ear.

He and Elenya exchanged a worried glance.

"Does *anyone* know we're in here?" she weakly asked.

And as if responding to her cue, the sun-stretched silhouette of their new neighbor once again appeared in front of the window— an eclipse so sudden it caused both Elenya and Myles to gasp. Brad like a statue. Brad like the moon. Brad's big ole head blocking out the rest of the cityscape as he pressed his dopey face against the opposite side of the glass.

"Whoa doggie, what's going on in here?" he said, squinting into their apartment. "You lose your shirt, big boy? Haha. Nah, I'm just playing. I know how you newlyweds are. You guys getting your mid-morning swerve on or what? A little noon-time nuptials, are ya? Dippin' your chocolate in her peanut butter, you ole dog? Haha. But seriously, are you guys having sex? Because I can come back if you're having sex . . . "

But he didn't leave.

He just squinted harder.

VIII

BRAD FROM NEXT door arched an eyebrow across his forehead, and his breath like a tea kettle steamed up the already-cloudy glass.

"So what the hell is going in here?" he said. "I heard a buncha shoutin' and bangin' around. Thought maybe y'all took a tumble or something. Was worried I'd find ya both bleeding out on the living room floor. A botched murder-suicide, perhaps? These things happen all the time. But not to worry, neighborinos. I know CPR. You hear that, Ellie? I can administer CPR to you if you need me to." He winked at her. She instinctively recoiled. His gaze drifted back to Myles. "I wouldn't call myself a 'hero' exactly, but I like to think I'd rise to the occasion if push came to shove."

"You have no idea how good it is to see you, Brad," Myles said. "We're actually in a lot of trouble here. We need your help."

"Of course, Myron. That's what neighbors are for."

" . . . Myles."

"Miles of what?"

"No, my name is Myles."

"Yeah. I know. That's what I said. MYLES. Now whaddaya all need'ta borrow a cup of sugar or somethin'? Haha."

"Can you call the landlord and tell him what's happening here?"

"You want me to call the landlord?"

"Yes. Please. The landlord. The police. The fire department. The fucking National Guard. Honestly, I don't care who you call. We're trapped in here and the mold is making us sick. The door is sealed from the inside and our phones stopped working and I don't think anyone can hear us unless they're standing directly on the porch like you are now."

"Well, that's not true. I can hear you both from my apartment next door, clear as day. That's actually why I was comin' over here now. Was hoping maybe y'all wouldn't mind keepin' your voices down?"

"What are you talkin' about?"

"The screamin'. Y'all need to stop screamin'. The walls are thin. It's very inconsiderate."

"What . . . "

"Look, MYLES, I know you're new to the building an' all, but we kinda have this unspoken rule about the noise levels 'round here. We ask everyone to try an' keep it down, especially between the hours of 10pm and 7am. We like to refer to as *quiet time*."

"I'm sorry but what the FUCK are you even talking about?!" Elenya was trying to keep her cool. She was so angry she was shaking. Myles could feel her vibrating. Like an idle car engine ready to shift into gear.

Brad gave her a bemused look. The kind of look a parent might give a child in the middle of a tantrum. When he spoke again, he spoke slowly, over-enunciating his words, like she was too stupid to understand them.

"It's a courtesy thing, Mrs. DeNova. Like don't start vacuuming in the middle of the night, no wild parties, etc. Some people have to work in the morning. Not everyone can sit around half-naked in their apartment all day."

He winked at Elenya once again. She tightened her robe in response. Fuckin' creepy bastard. And he wasn't even listening to her. Couldn't he see that they were in trouble? She wanted to throttle his neck. She wanted to bark in his face. But no. She kept her mouth shut. She ground her teeth and balled her fists and tried not to boil alive in her own blood. Myles was right. They *needed* Brad's help. Brad was the only one who could help them. And things were certainly tense enough as it was. She was trying her best to not let this "friendly" conversation devolve into something more acrimonious.

And then there was a *crack* inside of her head, so loud even Myles heard it. He turned to his wife. Her angry expression was immediately replaced by one of wide-eyed concern, like *oh shit, was that what I think it was?*

Jagged shards of broken tooth slipped out of her pursed lips.

Plink plink plink, like bloody porcelain against the floor. The inside of her cheeks was instantly shredded to pieces. Elenya couldn't even blink without further cracking the enamel.

Myles took her hand into his and gave it a little squeeze.

Her eyes were wet and desperate and wide, and with a begrudging nod she slowly opened her mouth and let her husband look inside.

Myles was met by eggshells. Her teeth were awash in a tide of spit and claret, left ragged like the rocks on some scabrous shore. In the newly-formed gaps of her once perfect smile a bunch of small, oval-shaped mushrooms had already begun to sprout.

Elenya held her breath as her husband reached into her mouth, and with a gentle but determined hand, plucked one of the toadstools out by the trunk—an impromptu dental procedure that fell somewhere between landscaping detail and a root canal. Elenya winced, raw nerves exposed, drool running down her chin. Myles held the tiny bloody mushroom out to his wife like it was some kind of perverse tulip.

She looked at it with abject horror. Looking at things with abject horror was becoming an increasingly frequent occurrence in this apartment. Myles turned to their neighbor who had watched this whole vile scene unfold with an abject horror all his own.

"Why don't I go call someone for you guys . . . " Brad said. And he disappeared from the window. *Poof.* Gone as quickly as he appeared. And yet, the DeNovas felt no absolution. Instead, a sense of dread purveyed the scene, as apparent as the air they breathed. They weren't out of the woods yet. In fact, they'd only just entered.

"What the hell is happening to us?" asked Elenya.

"I don't know. But we're gonna get to the bottom of it. Soon. I promise you, this will all be over with by this evening. You'll see. I need you to be strong. To keep it together for a little while longer."

"Keep it together? My fucking teeth are falling out."

"Yeah. I know. But it's not the end of the world. We can get you better teeth. Bigger teeth. Newer teeth."

"I don't want bigger teeth, Myles. I want MY teeth. I want to get out of this stupid apartment and get on with my life. We should've known better. We should've never moved here."

"Yeah, well, financially-speaking, we didn't have much choice.

That is, unless you got some secret savings account I don't know about. This was the place, El. This was the *only* place."

Elenya looked mournfully toward the empty window. Beyond it, the muffled sounds of the city grew dimmer by the second, replaced by the sounds of Brad rustling around next door. She shook her head like she was trying to shake off a chill.

"I don't trust him," she said.

"Neither do I," Myles replied.

"What do we do?"

"What *can* we do?"

She plopped down on the couch. The weight of her body sent another cloud of spores into the air, swirling around them in van Gogh-esque zephyrs. They would've had to stop breathing completely to not breathe them in. Mold in their lungs. Mold in their bloodstream. Mold filling in the folds of their brains like glue. Perhaps this was a problem fresh air wouldn't fix. Perhaps this was the kind of damage that couldn't be undone.

"Oooh, hold on a sec, I think I got an idea!" Myles suddenly lit up.

He disappeared into the kitchen and returned a few moments later with a pair of wine glasses and a gallon-sized jug of white vinegar. He placed the glasses on the coffee table and filled them both up to the brim.

"What are you doing?" she asked as she picked it up and gave it a sniff, so pungent it burned the inside of her already raw nose. Not quite a merlot, that much was certain. "Are we supposed to drink this shit?"

"Yeah. Vinegar. It's like . . . a *disinfectant*, right? I figure if we drink this it'll maybe help flush out our systems?"

"Flush out our systems?"

"Kinda a long shot, but what could it hurt? It's basically deconstructed salad dressing if you think about it. And salad dressing is delicious." He raised his glass. Toasted his wife. "Bottoms up."

Elenya raised the wine glass to her lips, but before she could take her first sip, she saw Brad once again looking in through their window like a creep. She let out a yelp.

"Jeezus, Brad, you scared the shit out of me! Again!" she said.

"Huh? Oh, yeah, sorry 'bout that."

"Maybe you can give us a little tap on the sill next time you're poking your head up, eh? I know you're trying to 'help' but it feels kinda like an invasion of privacy."

Brad shrugged noncommittally. "Look lady, if you're really worried about it, maybe you should hang some curtains up or something?"

"Right. Well you can bet that'll be the FIRST thing we do when we finally get the fuck outta here. I'll have 'em stop at Target on my way to the ER."

"So did you call the landlord or what?" Myles asked.

"Oh sure," Brad replied. "He didn't answer the phone but I left him a nice long message. Told him things're gettin' a little outta hand over here at the ole homestead. I said, send out the goon squad and have 'em bring the flamethrowers."

"Flamethrowers?" said Myles.

"Yeah, like in *The Thing*? You ever seen *The Thing*?"

"The Carpenter movie?"

"Hell yeah, the Carpenter movie. It's one'a my favorites. Kurt Russell. Keith David. Wilford fuckin' Brimley. All trapped together with that shapeshifting alien, pickin' 'em off one by one. The only way to kill it is with fire, remember?"

"I'm sorry but did you actually get in touch with anyone or not?" Elenya said. Brad shot her a disapproving look which he quickly covered up with a gummy smile.

"As a matter of fact, Mrs. DeNova, I did. After I left a message with the landlord I gave 9-1-1 a ring too. They had me file a police report and told me they were gonna send someone over first chance they got."

"Ohthankgod," she said in one big, breathy sigh. It was as if a weight had suddenly been lifted. The relief both she and her husband felt was incalculable.

"Don'tchu worry your rapidly-deteriorating little heads, neighborinos. I don't know if you can see from where you're sittin' but I brought my lawn chair and a sixer of Hamms. I'mma set up right here on the stoop and keep y'all company. I'mma make sure nothin' else untoward happens in the interim."

Brad unfolded his chair and nestled his butt into the well-worn grove. He cracked his first can, slurped the fizz from the top, and let out a sonorous and satisfied *ahhh*.

"I gotchu two," he said. "I'm your man."

IX

THERE WAS ONCE a river that ran through this city like a giant pulmonary vein through some kind of monstrous heart. It had long since dried up, according to Brad. Over a hundred years ago, he said. Well before any of them were born. But when it used to flow, it flowed mightily, he said. It was once the biggest river around.

The indigenous people called it the Sasquahatchee.

"Sas-KWA-hatch-EE" was how he pronounced it, hanging a half-second longer than necessary on each syllable, like he was reciting a poem. "It's an old Indian word, I think. Means escaping waters . . . or something like that." He chuckled to himself. "Of course, the only water escaping the city now is down in the sewer, fulla shit and piss."

It'd been several hours since Brad pulled up his chair. He finished his entire six-pack and was more than halfway through another. Nearly a dozen beers deep and showing no signs of stopping. He hadn't even gotten up to pee.

The cops still hadn't arrived. Whatever was holding them up, the DeNovas had no idea. Myles could hear police sirens wailing in the background. Just a din, beyond the walls. It was Friday night and there were probably plenty of "real" crimes being committed out there. Grand theft larceny. Assault. Rape. Murder. These kinds of things happened every day. Myles figured the cops must've had their hands already full. A couple of wannabe yuppies with a mold problem certainly wouldn't be their primary concern.

Wait, Myles thought. Was it Friday? Or was it Tuesday? For the DeNovas it was getting tougher and tougher to keep their timeline straight. Elenya decided it must have been Friday because it FELT like a Friday, like something BIG was about to happen, though if pressed she wouldn't be able tell you what.

Glassy-eyed Brad opened a fresh can and drank half of it down in one gulp. Continued to talk as animatedly as ever, rambling with the confidence of a museum tour guide and the apocalyptic fervor of a pickled street preacher. Brad was overflowing with historical facts and personal philosophies, as impressive as they were banal.

"Those who don't learn from the past are doomed to repeat it." He cast an arrogant eyebrow in their direction, as if he were waiting for them to praise his insight, as if he were the one to coin the phrase. "The sun goes down and the sun comes back up, but it's just an illusion. The sun stays in the same place. We're the ones who can't stop moving. Like the Mighty Sasquahatchee. The Dried-Up Sasquahatchee. Startin' upstate and flowing down through the pines. Alla this used to be unincorporated land. A few lonely houses scattered about here and there. Otherwise it was trees as far as the eye could see. It belonged to no municipality. Was claimed by no town. This place was once mysterious and inaccessible and full of promise. And now it's just a buncha shitty high-rise buildings that all look the same."

Sip.

"I used to be an architect. Didja know that? I used to work for the biggest firm in the state. Had my own office and everything. I'mma tell you this, nothin' I ever designed looked like one of those grotesque condos takin' over this city. My designs had *personality*. They were fuckin' human."

Sip.

"'Course those fuckers at my old firm wouldn't know true artistry if it were beating them to death with their own shoes. They canned me shortly after Jennifer left. Talk about insult to injury, amiright? They said it was my drinkin' but I know that's bullshit. I never let the drinkin' affect my work. Buncha Puritans, I'm tellin' ya. Nobody knows how to have a good time anymore. Jennifer too. She told me I had a problem. Told me to get help. And then she was out. Shiiiit, sometimes I think the whole world has their head on wrong an' I'm the only one who can see things the way they really are."

Elenya and Myles huddled on the other side of the glass, quietly sipping their drinks as well. White vinegar like cheap wine, burning as it went down, so painful they were on the verge of tears. Brad was on the verge of tears too, though his were of the besotted variety. Apparently, his separation from this 'Jennifer' person had not been amicable.

"Y'all just got hitched, so I'll spare you the bloody details, but marriage is like—umh—it's like a houseplant. You think *it's just a plant, it don't need much attention, a little water, a little sun, it'll mostly take care of itself.* Well, sure enough, you stop thinkin' about it . . . until one day you wake up an' discover it's already dead."

Indeed, Elenya's houseplant was already dead. Choked out and half-dissolved by the encroaching rot. Reverting back to the soil at the bottom of its pot.

Brad finished his beer. He opened another, lit cigarette stuck between his lips. The orange glow cast him in sharp, exaggerated shadows, like he was wearing a Halloween mask of his own face. Smoke danced around his head as the cherry burned down to the filter. He had already lit up another before that one was even out. Using them to punctuate his speech like a set of conductor's wands.

"In the end, I don't blame her for leavin'. It was my fault. I realize that now. I got comfortable in all the wrong ways. Took her for granted. Took everything for granted."

"Where are the cops, Brad?" Elenya asked. Her head thumped and her limbs grew stiff. She and Myles sat under the window, backs against the wall. The mold slowly advanced across the floor in front of them. "You said you called."

"I did call. And they're coming. I already told you that. Now shut up, I'm spillin' my guts out over here. I'm tryin' to tell y'all something important. Stop. Fuckin'. Talking."

What choice did the DeNovas have? The authorities were on their way, Brad kept insisting. They just had to wait it out until help arrived. They had no other choice. Elenya tried to find solace in the fact that at some point in the future, all of this would be no more than a memory, a nightmare faded to nothing under the cleansing light of dawn.

"Sometimes I like to pretend there's another version of us out there," Brad said. "Another version of me an' Jennifer an' everything we had, perfectly preserved, like insects in amber. A version of me unable to make the same dumb mistakes. A version of her that still loves me. That will always love me. Stupid thing to wish for, I know. But what can ya do? Every moment precedes the last. Hope is the errand of fools."

Sip.

"But y'all are big readers, right? Kinda a repeating theme in literature, ain't it? Love and longing and alla that jazz. Thought I saw you with that copy of *Don Quixote* earlier, did I not? Not quite a love story. Or is it? I'll be honest, I haven't read the thing. But you could do some serious damage with a big book like that. Bash someone's brains in, if you wanted to. Thwap. That'dbeya vegetable-maker, fer sure."

Sip.

"My point is, the choices you've made are the ones yer stuck with. Every passing moment is its own kinda amber. An' you can't go backward no matter whatya do. You gotta get it right the first time. Entropy is the natural order of things. Mountains erode. Stars burn out. And sometimes sayin' you're sorry ain't gonna cut it."

With the vinegar jug now empty, Elenya and Myles switched to whatever other moonshine they could find around the house. Windex. Lysol. A shot glass full of Drano, diluted just enough to not melt their insides completely. It was like a juice cleanse, except with a bunch of chemical solvents, and the more they drank, the more intoxicated they too became. It was placating, like alcohol, though not quite as stupefying, and spacey, like marijuana, though not quite as disassociative. This was a headspace that mollified the DeNovas. That relaxed them despite these dire circumstances. It was a kind of inebriation that felt wholly new.

Brad smiled knowingly. Or perhaps it was more half-knowingly? A quarter-knowingly? One-eighths knowingly? Whatever the case, Brad smiled at them in a way that suggested he knew a lot more than he was letting on. He had one of those faces. Used car salesman energy.

And the night continued. The night seemed to have no end. In the distance, sirens continued the wail. Ambulance. Fire department. The works. Flashing lights splashed the drab urban edifices around them in color—a parade to which they were not privy. No one showed up to help them. Perhaps no one *could* help them. Perhaps they were already beyond saving. Perhaps this was the end.

Brad slumped over in his chair like a snowman on the first day of spring as he got drunker.

HOUSE OF ROT

"Imagine if we were all born birds instead of people? That woulda been crazy, right? Me and you and everyone we know, just a buncha birds. Even ugly birds are beautiful. Pigeons and seagulls. Flyin' above the city. Doin' whatever we wanted. Free. Did'ja know a buncha crows is called a *murder*? Who decided that? Some sick fuck, I bet. The H. H. Holmes of ornithologist."

Much, much drunker.

"Sas-KWA-hatch-EE." Brad mumbled to himself, over and over, as if it were a mantra. Eyes half-closed. Breath slowing down. Head bobbing like a buoy at sea. The final beer had been finished, can already added to the pyramid of empties next to him. "They paved over it with the interstate. In a way, the river still flows, but now, instead of water, it's full of cars and trucks. We replaced the tributaries with on-ramps. The gyres with gridlock. That's progress for ya. Pave over the world. Pave over us too."

Indeed, factories and warehouses used to line the Sasquahatchee's banks like the backdrop to a Charles Dickens play. Now it was just a highway, though if you closed your eyes, the sound of traffic could still be mistaken for the *whoosh* of a rushing stream.

"Sometimes I wonder if anything we do or say matters," said Brad. "A century ago there was a river here. And in a century from now we'll all be dead. Every single human. Gone. At some point this apartment'll be torn down an' something new will be built in its place. The baton passed on. An' on an' on an' on. Sometimes it feels like we don't exist at all—the most infinitesimal parts in a machine so intricate it'll forever remain unknown. People are haunted, not just by the past, but by the future itself. What we could've been. What we'll never be."

The smoke from his nose encircled his head like the fog around a lighthouse. He managed to stand up on his gelatinous knees, each of his limbs slightly out of sync, like a marionette at the mercy of an amateur puppeteer.

"Maybe that's why people are so quick to believe in god," he said. "Even if we're playing a rigged game with an unfair judge, it certainly beats the alternative . . ."

" . . . and what's the alternative, Brad?" Elenya asked him.

He looked to the sky like he was trying to solve an impossible math problem inside his head before swinging his gaze back around to the sealed window and his imprisoned neighbors on the other side. Elenya raised an expectant brow, but he didn't have a clever answer for her.

He simply laughed.

X

BRAD EVENTUALLY STUMBLED back to his apartment. Elenya and Myles could hear him clunking and crashing about. He was right. These walls were paper thin. He flopped down on the couch. *Thunk.* Started to snore. *Zzz.* Only a few feet beyond this pimpled and pulsating veil, the wall looking meatier by the moment, the hallway like an intestinal tube, connecting their bedroom to the rest of the living space.

It was clear to the DeNovas that no one was coming to save them. At least not tonight. And probably not ever. Had Brad even called anyone? Did anyone but Brad know they were in there?

And yet the newlyweds stayed awake as long as they could, foolishly hoping that some outside force would intervene on their behalf. Some passerby with a keen set of ears would hear them. Some door-to-door salesmen looking to offload a set of encyclopedias would discover their imprisonment. Myles ready to shout, "Yes. Please. We'll take 'em, all twenty-six volumes, the whole dang alphabet, aardvark to zebra, just get us out of here!"

But in the end, exhaustion won out, as they knew it invariably would. They were vinegar drunk, insides asizzle. And like Brad next door, Elenya and Myles made their way to bed too.

The clock ticked past midnight. It was only the end of day two. Day fucking TWO.

And once again, in the darkness, the footsteps returned.

Elenya groggily awoke, head pounding like a timpani drum, stomach ready to lurch. Hot bile climbed her throat and into her nose, where it smoldered like fire. She turned to Myles, reaching out and placing her hand on his chest. It rose and fell in shallow breaths. He felt smaller, like he'd been partially deflated, and his flesh felt as damp and as pliant as papier-mâché. She could probably tear chunks off of him, if she wanted to.

Clomp. Clomp. Clomp. The sound echoed though the gloam. Their nightly visitors once again stomped around like they owned the place.

The footsteps and the fungus were related to each other, that much was clear. But the question was how? And why? And where were they going? And what did they want from the two of them?

Searching for some kind of answer, Elenya thought about her loving husband and her difficult neighbor and the faceless ghosts that occupied their twilight. She thought about the life she was promised yet still had left to achieve. She thought about all the people who had come and gone before her—the 100 billion human souls that somehow managed to claw their way out of the darkness only to quickly return, like they were never here at all. In the Great Grand Scheme of Things, she wondered what sort of impact any one individual could truly ever hope to have.

She thought about the unending chain of evolution, backwards through the eons and ages, to the beginning of time. The proto-human. The chimps and monkeys. The rats and squirrels and marsupials. The lizards and salamanders and fish and flatworms. And the fungus, the primordial muck, the puddle of nothing, the genesis of them all. Birth and death were conjoined twins, cosmically entwined, woven together by the rot. The whole planet was one big graveyard and her apartment was nothing more than a sepulcher within it. Everything was haunted. These footsteps have always existed. Elenya had just been too busy to notice.

She figured some kind of fever must've been working its way through her system. One thought melted into the next as her brain stewed in the cauldron of her skull. Oily sweat formed like pearls on the surface of her skin before soaking into the mattress underneath her, which aside from the stains from their excreted juices, had somehow been spared the mold. Elenya once again recalled the skinny salesman in his too-big suit, rattling off the features like he was reciting a prayer. Made with Silverflex™ foam technology, he had told them. Breathable. Firm. And, most importantly, *antimicrobial.* The word meant nothing to her at the time. Antimicrobial. Just a meaningless descriptor to justify jacking up the price.

But now their expensive new mattress was the only thing in this apartment left completely unscathed.

She opened her eyes. It was black in the bedroom, as it was the night before. She took a deep breath in. The air felt sharp in her lungs, a thousand scalpels.

Khak. Khak. Khak. She coughed so hard that something inside her broke loose. Like dice, she could hear it rattling around in her chest. Was it a bone? A muscle? Perhaps part of her spleen? Or was it something else? Some other kind of vestigial growth? Something that didn't belong there in the first place, rising up, to the top of her throat? Like magma in her esophagus, the pressure building so quickly she had no choice but to let it erupt from her mouth in a single psychedelic spurt. A dusty cloud of mushroom spores *khak*'d forth, the iridescent particles swirling through the darkness like she herself was a toadstool looking to spawn.

The spores slowly rained back down upon her. Neon confetti settled on the sheets, the floor, and the nearly-invisible figure standing at the foot of her bed.

Elenya nearly jumped out of her skin as the thing took shape before her—a network of fuzzy fibers filling in the empty space. Dim in the darkness, but still aglow from within. Long arms. Thin legs. Sloped shoulders. Ovular head. It was feminine yet featureless, like a department store mannequin, not quite human, but close.

Elenya curled up against the bed frame. Too terrified to scream. Myles continued to snore next to her, sleeping as soundly as ever.

The figure turned and left the room. *Clomp. Clomp. Clomp.* Elenya leaned over the edge of the bed. Mold in the shape of footprints sprung up behind each of its steps.

And as if compelled to do so, Elenya followed the thing, only a few paces behind. All of her joints felt like they were made of rusty hinges and her heart was racing so hard she feared it was going to explode out of her chest. If this were actually a dream, she wouldn't be in so much pain, now would she?

Elenya followed the ghostly figure into the living room, where it joined a second ghostly figure, wide and tall, broad-shouldered, square-jawed. She recognized him as the 'foreman' from the night before.

"Hello?" Elenya said.

Neither acknowledged her. They wove around Elenya like she was nothing more than an end table.

"Hello? Can you hear me?"

Still no response. And as they tread back and forth, a panoply of new rotten footprints rose up on top of the last, so lush the center of the room looked like an abscess. The mold consuming itself, consuming everything it touched. Turning into a puddle of slime, as black as tar.

"You said you were building me a castle. You said I *deserved* it. But things are only getting worse. No one is coming to help us. I'm rotting away."

They stopped and turned to face her.

No eyes. No mouths. No noses. Humans half-formed, their bodies a tangle of moldy filamentous strands, barely visible under the soft glow of streetlight coming in through the window. The two of them were like a rough draft of Adam and Eve. Their Garden of Eden in a perpetual state of decay.

Mildew coated the walls behind them as thick as skin, the photographs upon it like a series of tattoos—an illusion soon negated when her wedding photo suddenly fell and shattered against the floor.

Amid the moldy footprints, the photograph was cast, an ineffectual dinghy upon a roiling sea, drawn to the black spot as all things in the room were, past the clusters of mushrooms pressed to its murky shoreline, caps turned upward like daffodils facing the dawn. And as the photo drew nearer, the caps further unfurled, their hideous evolution not quite complete until they opened up into a crude set of fingers, one after another. Elenya could hardly believe what she was seeing. The living room transformed into an ocean of tiny human hands.

The photograph was torn to pieces. Turned into pulp. And she could feel the darkness feeding not only on the film base, but on her memory itself. These things were inexorably linked. There was mold in her brain, too.

Beyond the front door, the sun crested the horizon. It would be morning soon, and her two ghosts would be gone.

The taller of the two figures dropped to his knees in front of the black morass and spread his arms wide like Christ the

Redeemer. This was a symbol of peace. Of benevolent and willful surrender. Unraveling like a ball of yarn, he was both made and unmade by the mold. His body dissolved into a greenish-gray sludge, though it was clear these hungry hands could never be sated. These were his parishioners. This was his church. He was no longer a man-shaped thing. He was nothing. Gone.

The female figure followed suit. She held her arms out too, facing the morass.

"You don't have to do this," Elenya said.

The figure regarded Elenya with a curious tilt of the head. Elenya held up an open palm. A sign of goodwill. Please don't jump. I mean you no harm.

"You don't hafta haunt us. You don't hafta keep us trapped here. I could help you. Myles and me. We could both help you. I just need some kind of understanding. Why is this happening to us? Could you do that for me? Could you help me understand?"

The figure seemed to ponder the question. It stood stock-still as if in deep thought. It was roughly the same size and shape as Elenya herself, an almost mirror image, though the figure raised not an open palm in reply, but a single diaphanous finger instead, which it pressed to the center of Elenya's forehead.

A tingle passed through Elenya's body, followed immediately by a sensation of rapidly-increasing pressure on the inside of her skull. She felt both cold and electric as whiteness flooded her vision and her breath was sucked out of her chest. Ouf. And her head. Her head was going to explode. It felt like it was going to inflate like a balloon until it popped. Her brains would splatter the walls. Another midnight snack for the mold.

Oh lord, she thought. Oh Sweet Baby Jeezus. Oh no.

The world disappeared. It was like she'd been launched into space. The light at the end of the tunnel faded away. This place was far darker and far lonelier than she ever could've imagined. She waited for the chorus of angels to start singing. She waited to transcend to another plane of existence. She would keep waiting forever because there was nothing to wait for. She wasn't a ghost. She wasn't anything at all. Not even god could save her. Not that he cared. And her last thoughts flickered inside her head.

Hmm. So this is what it feels like to die.

DAY THREE

#firstworldproblems

XI

"**E**LLIE? ELLIE? JEEZUS. Elenya, wake up!"

The voice of her husband, like distant church bells, rang across untold distances, ferrying her back from unconsciousness. Elenya's eyes fluttered open.

She lay on the living room floor amid a surfeit of footprints, so multitudinous they formed a single mossy ring around her. Countless celestial bodies trapped in her orbit. She was Saturn, the God of Seed.

Blossoming out of the puddle of drool near her open mouth, a handful of exploratory toadstools probed her lips. Though no longer sprouting fingers, the mold continued to proliferate through dawn. Kitchen. Bathroom. Bedroom. Everywhere. There was not a single surface untouched by the rot, and it was still getting worse by the minute.

"Myles?" she said as he squatted next to her.

The joints in his knees popped like there was a war being waged beneath his skin. *Rat-a-tat-tat*. His chest appeared to be caving in and his back and shoulders looked as if they'd been rubbed raw. Blisters like constellations encircled his body, some ruptured open with what looked to be algae oozing out of the sores. What little hair he had left was greasy and glued sideways across his brow. Myles DeNova had the countenance of a broken thumb. It was like he'd aged thirty years overnight.

"Thank god." He exhaled a sigh of relief. "I thought you were dead."

Elenya felt tears welling up but found herself unable to cry. Mildew clogged up her tear ducts before spilling out into the white of her eyes. Her pupils floated like inner tubes on the surface of a scum-filled pond.

"Myles . . ."

"What the heck happened last night? Why are you on the floor?"

Her lip trembled. A structural weakness. Her face on the verge of collapse. How could she possibly explain to her husband what she went through when she barely understood it herself?

"I saw the future," she replied.

"What?"

"When I was passed out. I saw the future."

"Like . . . the *future* future?"

"Yes. No. I don't know. I saw the ghosts again last night. They woke me up. And I followed them in here. They're in the apartment still. In the floor. In the walls. In the mold itself. One of them *touched* me. And I was able to see what they saw, the universe unfolding in front of my eyes like a piece of origami. I saw death. I've been to the far end of the tunnel. The future isn't a place, Myles. It's an idea. There is no way to get there. The future only exists in our heads. A concept. An idea. Nebulous, at best. When we die, the future dies with us. That's what I saw. What I know. There is only this. Whatever this is. This apartment. Each other. This is the end of the line."

Myles took a deep breath and tried to process whatever-the-fuck that all meant.

"You know what I think mighta happened, El?" She raised an eyebrow. A weak cantilever barely holding up the rest of her face. Myles continued. "I think you mighta ingested too much of that toxic sludge and then hit your head when you fell down."

Once again, Elenya tried to cry but couldn't find the tears. No release. No relief. The mold had already taken so much, and it wasn't done.

"Fuck you, Myles. Are you even listening to me?"

Myles pushed the issue no further. This was not the time for debate. His wife needed him. And he needed to be there for her.

"Look, I'm in no position to play the skeptic, alright? I'm just trying to get a handle on the situation here. Same as you. Can you sit up?"

"I'm not sure," she replied as she wiggled a little. Not much leeway. The mold was functioning like an adhesive. The right side of her face was glued to the floor. Myles held out a helping hand

and Elenya used it to hoist herself upright, the pliant flesh tearing loose from her head with a wet, marmalade-like squish.

Oh no. No no no no no no.

Elenya looked down to see half her horrified face still glued to the wood. Mouth agape. Nostrils flared. One of her eyeballs had been yanked right out of her skull and left in a gooey pile, like a scoop of ice cream melting on a hot sidewalk.

She touched her cheek, fingers pressing into the exposed flesh. Myles choked back the vomit that was threatening to slither up his throat.

"How bad is it?" she asked him.

"You know those anatomical charts they have in the back of science textbooks that label all the tendons and bones and stuff . . ."

"Jeezus."

"Could be worse, though. You still got most of your hair."

"And I can still see out of it too."

"Huh?"

Elenya pointed to the eye stuck to the floor, its pupil a pinprick amid the bloodshot orb. Staring back up at her like a baby bird that had fallen out of the nest.

"You can see me out of that thing?!"

"That 'thing' is my eye, Myles."

"Sorry, I didn't mean to be insensitive. This is just . . . "

" . . . Disgusting? Weird? Impossible?"

"Yeah. All of those."

The eye strained and squinted until it was looking at Myles. He stepped between it and Elenya and tucked his hands behind his back.

"So how many fingers am I holding up?" he asked her.

She replied without hesitation. "Four. Now three. Now seven. Now four again. Aaaaaaand now you're just giving me the middle finger. Classy, Myles."

" . . . how . . . ?"

"I can *feel* the mold extending out of me, out into the room. It must be conducting information like fiber optic cables or something. It's like I'm woven into the carpet."

"But we don't have a carpet."

"Myles, we ARE the carpet."

Elenya plucked her eyeball out of the muck and wiped it off on her shirt before jamming it back into her head. It rolled around in the socket and settled into place.

The sustained wail of sirens beyond their walls cried—*waaahhh waaahhh waaahhh waaahhh*—like a nursery full of newborn babies demanding to be fed. It was triage out there, the DeNovas knew this, that was just the state of the world, and the paramedics and policemen were confronted with an endless series of emergencies, each one more pressing than the last. Gang violence. Sexual assaults. Shoplifting. Drug overdoses. Arson. Terrorism. Vandalism. Deadly pandemics. Chainsaw wielding maniacs. Credit card fraudsters. Traffic speeders. Black guys walking down the street, minding their own businesses. Cats stuck in trees. Teenagers skateboarding in places where there was a clearly posted sign that said NO SKATEBOARDING ALLOWED. This list went on and on. At least the DeNovas had a roof over their heads. Who were they to complain? Their suffering was only a first world problem.

"What happened to our couch?" Elenya asked, motioning toward the couch-sized lump of decomposing fungus draped across what was left of the wooden frame.

"It's totally gone. And so is your bookshelf."

She nodded to the coffee table. "Looks like *Don Quixote* survived. Which is good. I'm gonna get to it eventually. I swear."

The fuzzy gray layer that covered the floor grew ankle-high in some spots before erupting into either a bouquet of pink mushrooms or collapsing into a dark pool of reddish-black scum. The front door was completely gone. As was the window. As were most of the closets and anything else that used to be able to open up. Mold as thick as terrycloth covered the wall. Not even light could pass through. Thick ropes of jelly dripped from the ceiling to the floor. The room hemorrhaged around them.

The lamp in the corner flickered like it was sending out an SOS. Zaps of electricity could be heard buzzing through the apartment. Myles hit the power button on the television. Nothing. He tried it again. *Click. Click. Click. Click.* Nope. But the second he turned away, the screen suddenly lit up, bathing the room in light. Silvery and surreal.

"Lookin' for reruns of *Friends*?" she asked him.

Myles shook his head. "Shut up. I hate that fuckin' show."

He flipped the channels until he found news.

"I was thinking, what if it's not just us?" he said.

"What do you mean?"

"The rot. What if it's not just happening to us? What if it's happening everywhere? What if it's taking over, like some kind of *invasion* or something?"

"An invasion?"

"Yes."

"Like, what are you talking about? Aliens?"

"This isn't normal mold, Ellie. Or at least not like any mold I've ever heard of. What if it's some kind of *alien vegetation?* Can't those little fuckin' microscopic bear things survive out in space? What if it comes from space?"

"Bear things?"

"You know what I'm talkin' about. What are they called? The cute ones."

"Tardigrades?"

"That's them. Maybe it's a buncha tardigrades from fuckin' Alpha Centauri tryin'ta terraform the planet."

"Do you really think this is the work of a tardigrade, Myles?"

"Yes? No? What do you want me to say, Ellie? It's justa hypothesis. I mean, wasn't that a big plot point in *The Thing*."

"You and Brad really bonding over that stupid movie, are ya?"

"Ugh. Never mind. I'm gettin' it confused with *War of the Worlds* anyway."

"That's not the plot to *War of the Worlds* either, Mye."

Chip Honeycomb from the Channel Five News Team sat at his desk and faced the camera. Blonde hair in a perfect coif. Teeth as white as the virgin snow.

Chip gave them the rundown; a quick glimpse at the wider world. The top story was about some sorta humanitarian crisis developing in one of those sandy countries in the Middle East. Some sorta political upheaval was underway. Lots of collateral damage already. Grainy cellphone footage showed of a group of women and children fleeing from a bombed-out building. Men holding automatic rifles surrounded them, fingers on the triggers. This would not end well.

Myles squinted and thought, maybe that wasn't the Middle East after all. Maybe it was Africa. Or Mongolia. Or Utah. He couldn't say.

"The rest of the world doesn't seem too worried about the mold, Myles."

"No, I suppose they aren't."

The picture suddenly flashed like a strobe light and the colors inverted. The image on screen distorted as cracks formed along the glass. Chip looked like a pixelated monster as the LCD succumbed to the fungus now spilling out of the vents on the side of the set. *Zzst.* Contrails of smoke rose as blisters of mold dissolved the plastic, globs of molasses-thick spume cascading down to the floor. The TV went the way of the couch and the bookshelf before it. It broke apart into pieces which melted into the black gunky sludge in the middle of the room. Only a few spoiled bits remained.

Then the rest of the electricity in the apartment went out as well.

XII

THE POWER WASN'T coming back on. The apartment was falling apart. And the DeNovas were falling apart within it.

Myles lamented his lack of practical skills. He wasn't a good handyman. He couldn't play basketball. He'd never been in a fight. He didn't know how to change a tire. He was supposed to know how to fix things. That was how people were supposed to measure the value of a man.

An hour ago he went to take a piss and his penis ruptured open along the length of the shaft. Urine oozed out of the lesion as thick as tree sap before a floret of fresh fungus clogged it back up like a stopgap. His bladder ballooned up so large it looked like he was pregnant. And he still had to go. So he jammed what was left of his toothbrush into his urethra to try and reopen the passageway, but the pain was excruciating and he gave up halfway through. Another failure in a lifetime of failures. His dick was useless. He had no aptitude for home repair. He opened the circuit breaker and looked inside and it might as well have been the cockpit of a 737 for all he knew. Switches. Buttons. Some tube-shaped spark plug-looking things. Whatever they were they were covered in mold. Like everything else in this godforsaken place.

"We should try an' salvage whatever food we have left before it turns," Myles suggested as he and his wife entered the kitchen. Hopefully the seal on the fridge was enough to keep out the rot. He cracked open the door and they were immediately hit by a wave of thick brown muck. All of the contents inside had been digested. Liquefied. It puddled like wet shit around their feet. Elenya covered her nose, but it did little good. The stench was so powerful it felt like an extension of her own body. An extra appendage. As real as her toes.

Myles tried the sink, twisting the knobs as far as they'd go. The pipes wailed within the walls and then more shit came sputtering out of the faucet. *Frrt. Frrt. Frrt.* Filling the basin with crap. It wouldn't even drain. He turned off the tap.

"No food and water then?" said Elenya.

Myles shook his head. "What about those cans of beans we were throwing around yesterday? Those motherfuckers don't expire for like five years. They gotta be around here somewhere . . ."

"Look Myles, I'm not about to start crawling around on my hands an' knees looking for leftover Spaghetti-Os buried in this slop. We both know we aren't gonna find anything anyway, so who are you *really* trying to fool here, huh?"

"Okay fine!" he threw up his hands. "Fuck it. We don't need refrigeration. We don't need modern plumbing. And we don't need no busted-ass cans of baked beans either. We'll hafta figure something else out. Like . . . um . . . maybe some of these mushrooms are edible?"

"I think *we* might be the ones who are edible, Myles."

"You scoff, but what the fuck do we know, huh? This is a forest ripe for foraging. Some of these things could be tastier than chanterelles. Or finer than truffles. We could be sitting on a culinary goldmine here and not even know it."

"I seriously doubt that."

"Listen Ellie, uncommon problems require uncommon solutions. We gotta think outside-the-box. Now c'mon. Give yourself a little taste. Lemme know if it's any good."

His eyes were both wild and imploring, and Elenya begrudgingly plucked a single mushroom from the spot where her left bicuspid had once been and swallowed it down. It fizzled like cola as it bounced around in her guts. *Burp.* A plethora of fresh spores wafted out of her nose and mouth and pollinated her face. More fungus blossomed and once again filled her mouth like spongy teeth. She picked out her new bicuspid and swallowed that one down as well, with the same results. An endless cycle. She was regenerating faster than she could cannibalize herself. She supposed that meant they could survive on their own vegetation indefinitely, though whether eating yourself was a nutritionally viable option or not had yet to be determined.

"How is it?" he asked.

"Kinda bland," she said. "And I'm still hungry."

Myles frowned. He too was suffering his own unique form of mushroomification. They formed like soapsuds around the rim of his nostrils, curled out of the corners of his eyes like ivy, and sprouted out of his ears in two large stalks like Shrek. The side of his head where his hair first fell out now appeared as if it'd been splashed with acid. Bumpy and blistered and red. To Elenya it looked like part of his brain was exposed, a fresh sheen of lichen forming within the folds. He ran a finger through it and gave it a little taste himself. Yeah, it could definitely use some salt, he thought.

"Okay, clearly this isn't a best-case-scenario type situation we've found ourselves in, but we still got options. We just gotta think outside of the box that surrounded the box that we were thinking outside of before. We're only two boxes removed. That's not so bad, in the grand scheme of things."

"What the fuck are you talking about?"

"I'm sayin' let's take a deep breath an' try an' put things into perspective."

"I literally CAN'T take a deep breath, Myles. My lungs are only functioning at, like, 40% efficiency. It feels like an anvil pressing down on my chest."

"Okay, so take a FIGURATIVE deep breath then, Ellie. This is just a hiccup. Another minor setback. We both knew things were gonna be tough. Maybe not *this* tough. But still. We said it when we signed the lease. We'd scrounge and save for a few years. We'd build ourselves a little nest egg. We'd work hard and *earn* the spoils. That was the deal. Then we'll be able to get that house in the burbs. The one we always talked about. The one we were promised. White picket fences. Swing set in the back. That whole jazz. We'll have some kids. Start our family. Start our life. We'll subscribe to ALL the best streaming services and still have enough left in the savings to spend a week at Disney World when the summer rolls around. We'll build our portfolios. That's a thing people do, right? Build portfolios? We'll contribute to our 401ks. We'll plan for the future. We'll do it right. We're still young, Ellie. Well . . . we're still young-*ish*. We just gotta keep at it. Keep pushing forward. Keep playing the game, despite the setbacks. It's like Tennyson once said: 'I get knocked down. But I get up again. You're never gonna keep me down.'"

"That's *Tubthumping*, Myles."

"What does that mean?"

"That stupid quote. It's not Alfred Lord Tennyson. Those are the lyrics to the song *Tubthumping* by Chumbawamba."

"Chumbawamba?"

"Yes."

"You sure?"

"Yes I'm sure."

"Well, whatever. It's still applicable."

"So what are you gettin' at, Myles? That I shouldn't be worried? We're falling to pieces. We've been falling to pieces since the day we moved in here. You keep talking about the future. Our plans. Our hopes and dreams and all that other bullshit. I've already been there, Mye. I've seen the last page of this book. And it does not end well."

"No. You're wrong, Ellie. I don't care what you think you saw. We will get the things we've been promised. We'll replace our busted TV with a big ole high-definition flat screen. We'll both live until we're very, very old. We'll spend the rest of our days eating beluga caviar and wagyu beef. I have *faith* that everything is gonna work out in the end. And I'm not about to let one little refrigerator full of diarrhea stand in my way."

"I'm not greedy," she sighed. "At this point I'd be content if we could get the electricity back on."

He dismissed her with a wave of the hand. "This ain't nothin'. Think of all the people suffering all over the world. Think of the starving babies in Somalia and wherever. We've been coddled thus far. Coddled our whole lives. Alfred Lord Tennyson didn't have electricity. And we don't need electricity either. Most of these mushrooms seem to be glowing anyway. In fact, I can see just fine. What do they call that again, when a plant or animal makes its own light? Ya know, like a lightning bug or that ugly-ass fish with that bulb thingy danglin' in front of his face?"

"Bioluminescence?"

"Yeah. Bioluminescence. That's it. It's a good way to save on the electric bill, if you ask me. I certainly won't be bellyaching when the next payment comes due. You even seem to have a bit of a glow yourself. An Ellie-shaped figure cut out of the darkness."

"I'm glowing?"

"You're radiant, my dear."

Elenya shook her head. What a cornball. He smiled at her and she smiled back, but at the same time she couldn't help but pity her husband. Was this obtuse little pep talk all he had to give her? Yikes. It was as pathetic as it was insulting. And it was completely ineffective as well. She didn't want wagyu beef. She didn't even know what wagyu beef was.

"I wanna show you something," she said to him as she took his hand and led him out of the kitchen, stippled skeleton fingers wrapped up in a fist. Their various bacterium mingled.

They sloshed back into their unkempt fish tank of a living room. Everything they owned was already rendered into slop. This was their bog. Their entire world.

"I want you to see what I saw," she said to him. "To know what I know. I want to help you, Myles. But I don't know if I can."

"Help me?" he said.

Elenya positioned Myles at the edge of the obsidian pool. It was just wide enough to swallow the whole apartment. You could feel the pull of it, the increased weight, like you were carrying rocks in your pockets.

"Stand here and keep your eyes pointed down into the hole. Surrender yourself to the hole. Allow it to wash over you. Allow yourself to let go. For once in your life. For maybe the first time in your life. Stop fighting. Stop planning. Stop trying. And let go."

Toadstools like tiki torches bathed the room in red. The clotted expanse took up the floor, climbed the walls, and streaked down the halls. Myles did what his wife requested. He looked INTO the darkness. He looked THROUGH the darkness. He BECAME the darkness, much like his wife did the night before. He BECAME the abyss into which everything would eventually fall. Their furniture. Their appliances. Their ragged and unread copy of Don Quixote. Their clothing. Their food. Their fingers and toes. Their hopes and dreams. Their plans. Their future. Their sense of time. Their sense of self.

Nothing would survive this moment. There were no other moments. This was the beginning and end of everything. Like a dying star. A quasar. A black hole. She showed him what was on the other side of oblivion.

And a feeling of horror blossomed in Myles anew. Elenya could instantly see the change come over his misshapen face. It was like the moon eclipsing the sun. His heartbeat quickened. She could feel it pumping through the mycelium. Pumping through her body as well. The same blood that flowed through him also flowed through her and it flowed all around them like the Sasquahatchee River once did. There was nowhere to run. Nothing to escape to. No place left to go. She and He and this House of Rot.

All one.

XIII

All was silent.

And all remained silent.

This time, there were no footsteps. No more ghosts left to interrupt their slumber. Nothing except for the sound of Elenya blinking, echoing like the click of a camera shutter. The newlyweds lay next to each other on their fancy new mattress—their final resting place atop their final possession—left intact thanks to the antimicrobial miracle of Silverflex™ foam. Mildew glowed like the dawn that would never arrive. The question was no longer how long they'd been there, but if they'd truly ever been anywhere else. The two of them were on the other side of eternity. Like mummies in a sarcophagus. The King of Nowhere and the Queen of Nothing.

All was silent.

And then the tintinnabulation of a piano once again.

"My dear Elise/I am so pleased/Can you bring me/Some nacho cheese/And I must say/That I feel great/Doritos are/So taste-tayyy."

Myles was drawn backward; back from whatever precipice he'd been suspended over. Back into these horrid surroundings, Beethoven rattling through the walls. The fungus sang along, amplifying the music like surround sound speakers.

"Doritos . . . " The word came out slurred. His tongue was barely attached, much less at his command. And still, it was as if the eponymous Elise herself were administering CPR to him, pulling him out of his trance. Back into this moment. This inescapable moment, trapped in this apartment. The rumble in his tummy. His basest and most human of needs unfulfilled. "I'm hungry," he finally said. "And I want COOL RANCH DORITOS."

The record scratched. Music off. There was only the sound of

DANGER SLATER

Brad stumbling around next door. Their drunken neighbor poured himself a few fingers of whiskey, smacking his lips as he took a satisfied sip. He told them he'd called the landlord. Told them he'd called 9-1-1. Maybe he did, and maybe he didn't. Either way, the results were the same. Brad fulfilled his role. He played his tiny part in this story with aplomb. Now it was time to retire. Time to kick back his heels and let nature take its course.

Myles bolted upright so suddenly it shocked Elenya out of her reprieve. She followed his lead, bolting upright too. She was so close to disappearing. They were both so close to disappearing. The future extended no further than this moment. They were supposed to disappear. They should already be gone.

They climbed out of bed, bones as brittle as balsa wood. Joints like saloon doors creaking in the wind. These bodies weren't meant to stand. Yet they stood.

Two pairs of feet silently hit the mold-padded floor. Myles crept down the hallway. Elenya kept close. She was surprised her legs worked at all. When she looked down at her body she could see the mushrooms like modeling clay packed between her ribs. Filling her up. Filling her out. So full that the algae glooped out of her. Every orifice and every abrasion was a leaky sieve, but a few large vine-like stalks of fungus held her together. Weaving in and out of the fissures in her skin. Wrapping around her forearms and thighs. Taking on the form and function of her once-spoiled muscles.

She was almost made whole again. As was Myles. Just a glowing outline in the low light. He was a reanimated corpse testing out his newfound knees, wiggling his fingers in front of his face like he just discovered what they were. They'd grown nearly an inch since the last time he used them, five swollen toadstools lined up on each hand, caps pointed upward like little cruise missiles ready to launch themselves off her body.

They made their way to the living room, now a rectangle the color and texture of sanguineous flesh. Dozens of distinctive fungi bloomed. *Aspergillus* and *cladosporium*. *Trichoderma* and *stachybotrys chartarum*. Though they grew in different strains and bore different names, the grisly results were one and the same. Death. This was a room of death. No windows. No doors. Even the kitchen was gone, spilling into the main chamber, and Elenya and

Myles found themselves inside what could only be described as a hemorrhaging womb. Membranous walls. Viscera underfoot. Everything chewed up and regurgitated. It stank like rotten meat. It looked like a slaughterhouse, ooze dripping all around them like pus from a septic wound. Everything collapsing into the black spot in the center. This ever-growing maelstrom of tempestuous rot took up the near-entirety of the floor, a thin strip of fuzzy wood left for the two of them to maneuver around.

They shuffled to the far wall. A rusty nail still poked out of it where their wedding photo once hung. On the other side of it, Brad sat in his apartment. *Glug glug glug.* More liquor in his glass, then down the hatch.

The mold reached out. Caps opened up, each one comprised of five little digits. They rippled in waves, as if saying hidey-ho. Myles could feel them like they were his own fingers, his nervous system woven into the mycelium. He could make them flex. Make them give the thumbs up. Make them snap. Make them turn back around. Now a thousand tiny fists knocking on the gypsum that separated their apartment from the one next door.

Knock knock.

"Hey Brad. I know you can hear us."

Knock knock.

"WE KNOW YOU'RE IN THERE, BRAD. THERE'S NO USE PRETENDING YOU'RE NOT. WE JUST WANT ANSWERS. JUST WANT TO KNOW WHY."

"Myles, stop yelling. Isn't it supposed to be 'quiet time?'"

"Babe, I'm not fully convinced anyone else lives in this building besides the three of us." The mold knocked some more. "IF YOU HAVE SOMETHING TO DO WITH THIS BRAD, SO HELP ME GOD, I WILL TEAR THIS BUILDING TO PIECES WITH MY BARE HANDS. I WILL FIND YOU AND I WILL MAKE YOU PAY."

"You gotta calm down, Mye. Stop acting so aggressive. You win more flies with honey. Isn't that what they say? Watch and learn." She concentrated until she too was able to will the mushrooms to knock. Like raindrops. *Knock, knock, knock, knock, knock, knock, knock.* "NOW LISTEN UP BRAD, YOU IMPOTENT LITTLE BITCH, I'M DONE FUCKIN' AROUND. I WILL LITERALLY BURN THIS PLACE TO THE FUCKING GROUND AND KILL ALL OF US IF YOU DON'T ANSWER ME RIGHT NOW. ARE YOU

BEHIND THIS? IS THERE A WAY OUT OF THE BUILDING? ANSWER ME, YOU DRUNKEN FUCK."

Myles raised an eyebrow. "You call THAT honey?"

Elenya shrugged in response. "Shut up. I got carried away in the heat of the moment. Anyway, listen. It worked. He's moving around."

From the other side of the wall, a heavy thump, followed by the shuffling of feet as he bounced off the furniture. It was almost as if he were shocked to hear them. As if he were running scared. The DeNovas both yelled in unison.

"WE GOT NOWHERE ELSE TO GO, BRAD. WE CAN DO THIS ALL DAY."

"EVERY DAY."

"FOREVER."

"WE'LL KEEP SCREAMIN'. YOU'LL NEVER KNOW A MOMENT'S PEACE AGAIN."

He stopped running. Elenya and Myles shared an uneasy glance. Did it work? Had he actually listened?

The static click of a needle hit the groove of a record and all of a sudden, violins came at them like a cannonade.

Bum, bumbum, bumbum bumbum buh-BUM

Bum, bumbum, bumbum bumbum buh-BUM

The opening few bars to Mozart's *Eine Kleine Nachtmusik were* so loud and unexpected it nearly knocked Myles off his feet. He could feel the symphony moving through him in a mellifluous surge, setting his tenderest and most delicate parts aquiver. His heart raced. Thousand of outstretched fingers surrounded him, standing erect. This symphony licked the apartment like a giant tongue. Mushroom tips erupted in milky geysers of foul-smelling syrup, bukakkeing the DeNovas, who themselves could feel the pressure mounting within, like their bodies were teapots starting to boil, and then—*BOOM!*—they were excreting all over themselves as well, a spontaneous and uncontrollable toe-curling discharge, dripping from every pore.

"Oh god," said Elenya as she gasped for breath. Myles too was moaning. Eyes rolled back. Excreting all over himself. Filled with shame.

The music continued to play as the two of them regained what little composure they had left. Elenya looked at her husband. His chest pumped in and out. The red rashy skin was even redder and rashier than before.

"Did . . . you just cum?" she asked him.

His eyes darted guiltily back and forth. " . . . No. Did you?"

She looked down at the gooey stain on the front of her crotch. " . . . No."

"Oh. Well good."

"Good."

"I think he's trying to drown us out," Myles had to shout as the music once again got louder. It was building to another crescendo. The fourth movement. The allegro.

"It seems to be working," Elenya shouted back. "I can barely hear you."

They had no other option but to continue NOT cumming in their pants until the otherworldly concert next door hit its frenzied and phantasmagorical final note.

And then all was silent.

And the newlyweds breathed a sigh of relief.

"Is it over?" Elenya asked.

And then *Piano Concerto No. 3* by Rachmaninoff started to play.

XIV

THE MANIC FINGERS of the Russian maestro pirouetted across the keyboard. Then entered the woodwinds, the goose-like ululation of oboes and bassoons. The rest of the orchestra soon followed suit, brass, percussion, and strings all working in harmony. Even the hiss of the phonograph seemed to match the beat.

Myles let loose a scream, cathartic and desperate and primal. So loud it caused his few remaining teeth to pop like pimples inside his mouth. The black spot in the center of the room bubbled up like a pit of molten tar. He could feel the gravity of it, clawing at him, trying to pull him down. To pull everything down. The apartment was disappearing into the darkness. And Rachmaninoff, for his part, provided them with what could only be described as an appropriately dramatic score.

Myles screamed again. Screamed even louder. Elenya could feel his scream in her body, as thick as her blood, as potent as alcohol. They were connected through the mycelium, supping from the same emotional pool, fear and frustration distilled down to their purest forms. And she watched her husband with a mixture of wonder and admiration as he stomped around the living room. An angry bear in a fleshy cave, looking for something to smash. Something to destroy. Something snapped inside of him. He was looking to fight in any way he could.

They'd been together for years. Dated for nearly half a decade before they tied the knot late last year. In many ways, she knew Myles better than he knew himself. She saw all the compromises he made in the service of convenience. Her husband, who always assumed things would work out on their own. Her husband, who always opted for the path of least resistance. She was guilty of those things, too. She knew that. That was why they rented this apartment. The first one they found. Things would be great, he promised her, though he had no basis to make such a claim. Just wait and see, he said. Wait and see.

But this rage he was expressing? This was more than a corpse like him should be able to muster. Oh yes. She could feel it awakening something inside of her, too. Rage meant passion. And passion meant hope. Overcoming the odds. Overcoming reality itself. Myles clawed at the Mini Cooper-sized polyp that used to be their couch and dug out handfuls of oily black fungus, and he flung that fungus around the room like a monkey flinging its shit. He was doing these things not because they were particularly helpful but because he COULD. He'd seen the future. Same as Elenya. The darkness. The pointlessness. The futility of it all. And still, he continued charging into the abyss. He wasn't gonna disappear without a fight. In the end, what more could you ask for?

"That sonofabitch," he growled. Clusters of white fuzz sprouted out of his skin like the fur of an arctic wolf. Hackles up. Closing in. Ready to attack. He motioned to the wall. Their neighbor somewhere beyond it. "That sonofabitch . . . "

"We have no way of stopping him, Myles."

"I know."

"We don't even know what he wants."

"I know."

"We can't stop the mold either."

"Ellie, I already know all this."

"So what *can* we do?" she asked.

Brad changed the record. Giuseppe Verdi. The second act from his Requiem. *Dies Irae*. The Day of Wrath. Once again, it was the perfect soundtrack to accompany this apocalyptic scene. What was the deal, Myles thought? Could Brad somehow see them? It seemed almost impossible he was choosing these particular songs at random. Why the hell did he own so many classical music albums anyway? Would it kill him to throw on some Bowie or something? Thematically-speaking, *Under Pressure* would work in this scenario just fine.

They were rotting apart at unprecedented speeds. Pearly ribbons of jissom ate through what little meat they still had. It was like they'd been blasted with lasers. All the filaments and fibers that once held their bodies together now unraveled, turning instantly gangrenous. Dripping black slime. His bones were as thin as Jello, and pieces of him fell to the floor. There went his arm. *Plop*. His nose. *Plop*. Both of his kneecaps. *Plop*. *Plop*. Elenya's stomach ruptured open, guts threatening to spill out. She managed to catch them and cradle them before any of the more important tubes tore loose. She slung the whole kit and caboodle over her shoulder. They still worked, but not very well, and probably not for much longer.

The newlyweds looked to the roiling black sludge taking up most of the floor. The world felt like one big wagon wheel. An ouroboros. A snake eating its own tail.

And then, the smallest of smiles appeared on Myles' cheeks. At first, Elenya thought she was seeing things. What the fuck could he possibly have to smile about? This was the end of the fucking universe right here.

"What?" she asked him.

"I have an idea."

"An idea?"

"Yes."

"Now?"

"Yes."

"You can see that I'm wearing my guts like a backpack, can't you? I think we might be past the point of ideas."

"Well it's not a very good idea, but considering the circumstances . . ."

"Oh my god, quit stallin' and out with it, Myles."

"I think we need to go in."

"Go in?"

"Into the black spot."

"What the hell are you talking about?"

"Think about it, Ellie. We're circling the drain here. We can keep running, but in the end, we're only delaying the inevitable."

"Good. Let's delay the inevitable then."

"Ellie . . ."

"No. It's just the fungus talking, Myles. I can hear it too. Begging me to let go. But we've both been down that tunnel before. We both know that the light on the other end is just an illusion. Once you disappear, you disappear forever."

"C'mon, hurry . . . " Myles said as the left side of his body started to bifurcate from the top down, right along the hemisphere between the two halves of his brain. His skull split apart like softened wax. He took his severed arm and jammed it like a spear through the side of his head, effectively holding himself together with it. Somehow the fingers on the end were wiggling. Beckoning Elenya to follow him back down the hallway. "We're running out of time."

The moss-covered walls in the bedroom grew so thick it appeared to have shrunk. Dimension-wise, it was now barely bigger than a closet. The ceiling sagged like a blood-filled blister. The newlyweds had to hunch to get inside.

"What are we doing?" Elenya asked.

He pointed at the mattress. Their only possession. A single strip of gauze on an incurable wound. "It uses Silverflex™ foam technology," he replied. "It's antimicrobial. It's immune to the rot."

"But so what?"

"Help me drag it out of here."

"Myles, no. I'm tired. My legs barely work. My sphincter is like three inches away from my nose. Can't we just lay down on it and go to sleep?"

"We can. Tomorrow. I promise we can die tomorrow. But for now, please grab the other side of it and help me hoist it up. It's too heavy to move on my own."

They slid the mattress off the bed frame with coordinated effort and slowly heave-hoed it to the living room at the other end of the hall.

Elenya was out of breath. The lungs on her back dripped like leaky bagpipes. All she wanted to do was rot in peace. Soon enough, she thought. Whatever this ridiculous plan was notwithstanding.

Black mold ate through the wood completely. The entire living room collapsed in on itself. Elenya and Myles stood on the edge of the chasm, feet firmly planted to keep from falling in too soon. A few hyphae like streetlamps provided them some flashes of dim light, though they too were disappearing into the darkness as the floor continued to crumble. The hole was getting wider and wider, though perhaps not quite as bottomless as Elenya would have assumed. She could hear the sound of rushing water down there.

It echoed throughout their apartment. Air whooshed around them, whipping the last few strands of her ratty hair in her face.

"A sewer line?" Elenya asked.

"I don't think so," Myles replied.

"You sure about that?" She took a big whiff. "It certainly smells like a sewer line. Though I could be mistaken. Like I said before, I'm still gettin' used to this whole guts-on-the-outside-butthole-positioned-not-nearly-as-far-from-my-nose-as-it-used-to-be thing."

"What was the name of that river Brad was talking about the other day? The one that used to flow through the city?"

"The Shasquatchy? The Squishyquanchy? Something like that?"

"The Sasquahatchee. That was it." He motioned downward. "I think this might be the Sasquahatchee River."

"I don't understand. There is no Sasquahatchee River. Not anymore, at least. It dried up a long time ago. Isn't that what he told us?"

Myles shrugged. "Maybe he was wrong?"

Brad switched the record. Tchaikovsky's *Swan Lake, Op. 20, Act II, Scene 10: Moderato.*

Myles said, "This song always reminds me of that one Taco Bell commercial from a few years back. Do you remember the one? It opened with that little fuckin' chihuahua mascot they used to have, sitting in the box seats at Lincoln Center, taking in the ballet. He wore a tuxedo and top hat and was somehow holding up a pair of small silver binoculars to his buggy eyes, the implication being that the Taco Bell chihuahua was an appreciator of not just the performing arts, but a creature of discerning taste in all sorts of culturally literate ways. Cut to: an usher quickly making his way through the halls of the theater, carrying a paper bag with the Taco Bell logo on it prominently displayed. All the high-society gourmands look on with envy. What beautiful genius thought to have Taco Bell delivered to the opera, they thought? Who among us could wield such power? The usher makes his way to the balcony. Pushes through the double doors. The stoic chihuahua glares at him, an expression of contempt on his tiny face, as if to say, what took you so long, you peon? My food better not be cold! The usher bows out of the room. The dog noisily pulls a

HOUSE OF ROT

Crunchwrap Supreme out of the crinkly bag and takes a single yet satisfying bite so loud and disruptive it causes everyone in the auditorium to turn around and look at him. The dancers onstage have stopped dancing. The musicians in the pit have put down their instruments. The conductor of the orchestra lets out a audible harrumph. The chihuahua takes a moment to savor the taste of it, then sheepishly turns to the camera and says, 'Yo quiero Taco Bell.' The ad break ends and we're back to watching old episodes of Two and a Half Men."

"I'm sorry, but WHAT are you suggesting we do?" Elenya asked her husband.

"I'm saying we roll ourselves up in this mattress like a Crunchwrap Supreme."

"You want us to turn ourselves into a Crunchwrap Supreme?"

"It's a metaphor, El. But yeah, that's about the long and short of it."

"And then you want to jump into this rotten hole in the floor?"

"The way you're sayin' it makes me sound crazy."

"You honestly think this mattress is enough to protect us?"

"I honestly have no idea. But at this point, what choice do we have?"

Elenya once again leaned over the edge. *Whoosh*. This certainly wasn't part of the future she'd envisioned. Wherever this tunnel led would be someplace new. Someplace unprecedented. Perhaps things would get better. Or perhaps they were about to get a whole lot worse. She was filled with trepidation, but ready to take that chance.

"I'm scared," she said.

"I am too," he replied.

He grabbed the side of the mattress and folded it around himself. She grabbed the opposite side and did the same. They rolled themselves up, bodies meeting in the middle. The two of them were a jumble of ground beef. She could feel his heart racing, just as he could feel hers. Syncing up. A single beat that the newlyweds shared. They kissed. A passionate and loving kiss. The fungus pollinated the space between their open mouths. Mold fused them together. This was an embrace from which they'd never be able to untwine.

The rest of the floor collapsed beneath them.

And into the Sasquahatchee River they plunged.

DAY ZERO

THE
MIGHTY
SASQUAHATCHEE

XV

THE **LIGHT AROUND** her was so bright it almost seemed unreal.

Blink. Blink. Blink.

It took all her strength to pry her eyes open. She breathed in deep. Fresh air.

Elenya DeNova found herself outside, awkwardly cast against the rocks on the river bank. The once-raging rapids slowed to a trickle. Birds chirped somewhere nearby. A sunbeam like a scythe cut through the canopy.

Groggy. Disheveled. Dirty. Bruised. Like waking up after a night of heavy drinking. She slowly pieced herself back together again. The who, what, where, when, and why of it all. She sat up with a start like she'd suddenly been resurrected from the dead.

Her clothes hung in rags. She wasn't wearing shoes. She wiggled the ten tiny digits at the end of her bare feet, one toe at a time, shocked to find them there. Shocked to find them functional. Her innards respooled themselves. Her arms and legs were reattached. Teeth filled her mouth. Hair covered her head. Her body was no longer decomposing. She was intact. She was healed.

She stood and almost immediately toppled back over. These were new muscles, after all, untested and unproven. But it was like riding a bicycle, the learning curve was not steep, and after a few rickety steps she could walk again.

She looked around. Trees in every direction. She wasn't within city limits. There were no signs of civilization anywhere. No houses. No trails. No people. Traffic did not rumble down distant highways. Contrails from planes did not checker the sky. Myles was nowhere to be found, either. Elenya was completely alone.

She retraced their steps, from Point A to Point B:

The mold had eaten through the floorboards. The entire apartment was swallowed up by the abyss. They fell into the hole. Everything fell into the hole. Elenya and Myles had rolled themselves up in the mattress like a human Crunchwrap Supreme. They plunged into the water. Into the murky depths below. They'd been told the river ran dry. But oh no. No no no. That wasn't the case. Not even close. The Mighty Sasquahatchee once again flowed, buried beneath the city. Now a runnel for all sorts of biological waste. Plasma and entrails and chunks of blood and brain matter. Bile. Mucus. Piss and shit. Every vile fluid a human being could produce, festering in the darkness, forming the slurry in which they found themselves immersed. The mold like a lubricant greased the walls around them. There was nothing to grab onto. The current took them.

The liquid soaked into the memory foam. Made the mattress so heavy it started to sink. Sludge sloshed over her face. Gagging on her words as she talked.

"Myles . . . ?" she sputtered

"I'm here," he replied.

"What do we do when the mattress is gone?"

"We hold onto each other."

"But my arms are like anchors."

"I know. Mine are too."

"So how do we stop ourselves from sinking?"

"I don't know if we can."

The stench of decay filled her nostrils and the taste of refuse settled on her tongue. The mattress was rapidly disappearing beneath the black water. If Silverflex™ technology wasn't going to save them, what would?

The mattress capsized. They were out of options. They had to let go. But not before Elenya reached down, pulled out a huge chunk of memory foam, and swallowed it in one bite.

Myles looked at her like she was crazy. And perhaps she was. Perhaps they both were. Perhaps eating the mattress was the only way they could take it with them. Perhaps that is where their salvation lay. Perhaps they needed to become ONE with the mattress all along. They'd already been baptized in shit. They'd already been born again. Perhaps the only thing left to do was allow their fancy new mattress into their HEARTS and SOULS. The

HOUSE OF ROT

DeNovas were in no position to engage in theological debate. Myles wasn't about to question her logic, nor would he question the logic of God. He too ripped out a handful of memory foam and swallowed it like a communion wafer. He accepted this mattress as his Personal Lord and Savior, Jeezus Christ. Amen.

Chunk after chunk, the DeNovas ate the entire thing. The memory foam filled them up like putty, stuffed into their fissures and caked around their bones. Their once-fetid internal organs were replaced by buoyant new ones, and their blood was pumping once again. Oh yes. They grew stronger with every bite.

And still, they were no match for the raging Sasquahatchee. They were at the whims of the rapids no matter how hard they swam. Myles reached out, trying to hold on to his wife. And Elenya tried to keep her husband in her grasp as well. But it was no use. These dark waters were meant to tear things apart.

The tunnel curved left. Curved right. Faster and faster. Elenya was tossed like a rag doll. There was no way of telling which direction was which. The mattress was gone. Her husband was gone. She called out his name and got no response.

Liquid filled her lungs. It soaked into all her foamy new parts, the weight of it forever increasing, pulling her downward. Too much to bear.

Her head dipped beneath the surface. There was no sound under the water except for the rush of the current around her. No light either, but the last flickering thoughts of her oxygen-deprived brain. At the bottom of the Sasquahatchee River there was darkness. She closed her eyes and went to sleep.

And when she woke up, she found herself alone on the shore, gasping for breath. The Sasquahatchee winnowed down beside her, now just a placid creek. Woodlands surrounded her in every direction. She had no idea how far she had come and no idea what time of day it was, either. Cloud cover diffused the sunlight. It was impossible to tell where its exact location was.

She felt itchy all over, like she was wearing a wool sweater under her skin. Had to be the memory foam inside of her drying out. But no matter. She'd made it out of the apartment. She was alive. This was a version of the future that defied her vision. This was a version of the future that probably shouldn't exist at all.

Yet here she was.

KKRAK

The snapping of a twig echoed like a gunshot. She whipped around and saw Myles standing there with his hands up.

"Don't shoot," he said.

She exhaled in relief. "Jeezus, don't sneak up on me like that."

"Sorry. Wasn't tryin' to. I was callin' out your name but you didn't answer."

"I didn't hear you. I think I got water in my ear or something."

She leaned to the side and shook her head. A trickle of warm water leaked out of her ear canal, along with a couple of wriggling grubs.

Myles watched the worms disappear into the dirt before turning back to his wife. "Well, other than whatever THAT was, you look good, babe. Like how I always picture you in my head. As beautiful as the day we were married."

"You look good too, Mye," she replied. "You look *healthy*. Even your beard isn't as gray as I remember it. And the mushrooms growing out of your ears are gone."

"I *feel* healthy, all things considered. Though I'm itchy as fuck."

"Oh sure. Me too. I think I got memory foam clogging up my arteries like cholesterol. But one problem at a time, right?"

"Right. First things first. Like maybe we should figure out where the hell we are."

"I was kinda hoping you recognized it."

Myles did a quick 360° and returned with a shrug. "Some kinda forest, I reckon?"

"Yeah. That's what I figured. Are you hurt at all?"

He rotated his shoulder. Wiggled in place. Winced a bit. "Yes. But I'll live. I mean, who am I to complain about a little shoulder pain when there are people in places like Azerbaijan who don't even have access to clean drinking water? What are we doing to help them, Ellie? Huh?"

"You can walk though, right?" she asked, ignoring his outburst, though she too felt guilty about not advocating harder for the Azerbaijani people. Maybe she could tweet @ her congressman when this whole thing blew over?

"Should be able to, yeah," he replied.

"Alright then. I guess we start walking."

XVI

ALONG THE RIVERBANK, they walked; the same
direction as the running water. South, Elenya figured. Most rivers
ran south. Though without a compass, this was merely a guess. The
newlyweds were simply going with the flow.

They didn't talk much. There wasn't much to talk about. You
could only say 'fuck' so many times before the word lost all
meaning. And they were fucking done with this fucking bullshit.
They were lost in the wilderness. For hours they trekked, passing
trees like the background of an old cartoon, a verdant landscape
endlessly repeating itself. They walked for miles and never saw
another person nor crossed a single road.

Perhaps they were dead, Myles thought. Perhaps this was
purgatory. Perhaps they would follow the Sasquahatchee forever.
Perhaps this was some kind of cosmic retribution. A balancing of
the scales. Despite all the advantages they'd been given, they still
clamored for more. For the lower-middle-class, there could be no
greater sin.

And upon that thought, a sound could be heard. Faintly rising
like the fog out of the stream. Elenya and Myles stopped and
listened. There was no mistaking it. The rhythm. Louder than the
river lapping against the bank.

"You hear that?"

"I do."

"Where is it coming from?"

"Somewhere in front of us, though its hard to tell."

"A flurry of piccolos."

"Yeah, those are piccolos, alright."

"And violins too."

"Myles, I think it's music."

Indeed it was music. *Peer Gynt Suite No. 1, Opus No. 46: Morning Mood* by Edvard Grieg to be exact. Though they were not as cultured as the Taco Bell chihuahua, Elenya and Myles still recognized the tune, if not by name, then at least by melody. Soft and mellifluous. The aural equivalent to warm light. This was sunrise music, cued up on the soundtrack to signify the dawning of a new day.

The acoustics out there were terrible, muted by the vegetation, sound dispersed among the endless copses of trees. But as they continued down the river they realized they needn't veer off the shoreline. It was getting louder. They were drawing near.

Coming upon a thicket of sorts, where the trees and bushes grew so dense that the DeNovas couldn't see through. But this was where the music led them. This was the way they were supposed to go. And though apprehensive, Elenya and Myles pushed forward through the brush.

They found themselves on an open piece of property with an isolated house positioned in the center. Though it had a driveway, there was no road nearby for it to connect. They were in the middle of nowhere. Nobody would build a house out here. It didn't make sense.

The yard was pocked by clumps of overgrown grass, and the white picket fence that surrounded the property had fallen into a bit of disrepair. Like feral animals, the DeNovas slowly approached, the music still playing, descending on them like rain. Not quite your typical two-story colonial, part stucco, part stone. It was as if the architect were trying to smash together two very different designs. Classic Americana meets the Middle Ages. Romanesque but with a few modern touches too. After all, no suburban home was complete without Central Air and Central Heat.

A single chimney rose like a spire. The house had walls like a battlement and windows like arrow slits. When Elenya squinted, it looked like a miniature castle. Yes. That was it. A castle the size of a suburban home. Even the Sasquahatchee seemed to acquiesce to the illusion, curling around the structure like a moat. A wooden walkway in front of the door crossed the river like a drawbridge. It was like in the princess books she read as a kid. Her castle. Her kingdom. Tears of joy welled up in her eyes.

HOUSE OF ROT

"It's just like how I always imagined it. Right down to the moat an' all."

"What the hell're you talkin' about, Ellie? You've seen this place before?"

"Come take a look around back." She grabbed him by the wrist and dragged him to the side of the house so they could see the backyard. "There's even a swingset already set up for the kids. For OUR kids, Myles. This is where they'll grow up."

"It's rusted to shit."

"But you can fix it, can't you?"

"Uhh, I suppose."

"Sure you can."

"But doesn't this all seem a little . . . strange to you, El?"

"Of course it's strange, Myles. Everything is strange. Everything has always been strange. But we finally made it. I can't think of anything stranger."

"But where are we, Ellie? Is this place even real?"

"I don't know. And I don't care. It feels like home. Myles, we're home."

The music suddenly stopped. The record scratched. *Fffwwwzzzppp.* Elenya and Myles whipped around to find Brad sitting in his lawn chair behind them, his open cooler within arm's reach, packed full of cold brewskis. His phonograph sat on the ground next to it, uncharacteristically silent. He ashed his cigarette into the speaker cone and exhaled smoke through his teeth. His head bobbled side to side. There were a bunch of empty cans around his feet. He'd already had a few.

"Brad???" Elenya was almost too shocked to speak. "What are you doing here? What the fuck is going on?"

Without the window between them, Brad seemed much taller. And in much better shape. He took another drag from his cigarette, dramatic and slow. His chest inflated, straining against the buttons, nearly bursting through his shirt. He pointed to the Sasquahatchee and gave them a gummy smile.

"I told'jall a river ran through here, didn't I?" he said. "Y'all doubted me. Y'all thought I was just some fuckin' drunk. Some loser. Well I guess y'all didn't know shit."

"You also told us you'd help us, Brad," said Myles. "You told us you were calling the authorities. You told us not to worry about the mold."

"Look man. I've been tryin' to help you this whole time. Since the day you moved. I've been talkin' an' talkin' an' yet no one ever wantsta listen to a guy like me. An' now it's too late. I mean, take a look around'ja, buddy. There ain't no one else here."

He pulled a beer out of the cooler and popped the top., slurping down half the can without taking a breath. He held up a cold one to Myles. Myles declined. Offered it to Elenya. She declined as well. Brad shrugged and put it in his lap. He'd get to it soon.

"I was an architect. Yup. I told'ja this. I used'ta build buildings all over the city. An' none of them were high-rises. Fuck the high-rises. I was tryin' to build something REAL. But all that was before Jennifer left. Back when she and I were just like the two of you. Still dreamin' bout the future. Still holdin' out hope that e'erything was gonna turn out okay. Heh. Man. Perspective is a funny thing. The end'a one thing. The beginnin' of another. Life is a series of cycles. Took me a long time to realize that. Maybe you evolve. Maybe you don't. Mosta the time it don't much matter. The scenery will shift along the way. But nothin' ever really changes. Not unless you do."

Myles rolled his eyes. "Ugh. Gimme a break, would'ja, Brad? No one cares about your stupid failed marriage, okay? No one gives a fuck about the jobs you got fired from. No one wants'ta listen to your ridiculous classical music albums. And no one here's got the time to decipher your drunken little riddles. You're stuck in the past, man. An' I'm not like you. WE'RE not like you. So you can either explain to us what the hell this is all about or you can get the hell outta our way."

Brad was taken aback, but only for a moment, and he refused to let it show. He finished his drink and tossed the empty. *Clank.* It struck some distant rock off in the bushes somewhere. This pastoral landscape was no longer untouched by man. Brad just invented litter.

A moment passed between the three of them. Smoldering and uncomfortable, like a petri dish under a set of hot lab lights. Something was happening. Some kind of decision was made. Not even the birds dared to disturb them. Nor did the river. The babbling Sasquahatchee babbled no more.

Brad slowly bent down, scooped up a handful of dirt, and held it out for them to observe. The pile sat crumbling like a pyramid in his open palm.

"Look close. You'll see it. Woven in'ta the soil. Threadlike. Thin. Like little lightning bolts. That mold you thought'ja were runnin' from? Well, I hate to break the news to ya, but there ain't no outrunnin' it. It stretches across the forest. Under our feet. Under the dirt. It's everywhere. It always has been. Beyond time itself. Travel as far as you want in either direction, you ain't gonna find nothin' but rot on either end."

The rest of the dirt slipped through the cracks in his fingers to reveal the button-shaped mushroom previously buried within. It was swollen and red, like an overripe apple, with a few white dots speckling the cap. It looked like something out of *Alice in Wonderland*. Brad held it between his thumb and forefinger. Presented it to Elenya like a corsage. She raised an eyebrow.

"What? Am I supposed to eat that or something?"

"Honestly, it don't make a difference what'chu do, Elenya. The universe don't owe us an explanation. The universe ain't even listenin'. A hundred billion people have come an' gone. Alla 'em disappeared into the void, still askin' the same ole questions. Still wantin' to know why. But who knows, maybe you'll be the first person in human history to figure it all out. What's the point of all this, you ask? Well shit, as far as I could figure, if you can't find meanin' in the question itself you'll find no meanin' at all."

Brad took the mushroom cap back and tossed it into his own mouth, only taking two chews before swallowing it down. The change in his countenance was almost immediate. His eyes unfocused. They found the middle distance, and the self-satisfied smirk he always wore slowly melted away.

" . . . Brad?" said Myles.

"Think I'm just gonna lie down for a minute, if'n you don't mind."

He fell out of his chair, muscles unable to hold their own weight. He flopped onto the ground, face down, entire body limp. Only able to shovel a few more handfuls of dirt into his mouth.

The back of his clothing had already rotted through. Raggedy fabric hung moist with slime. Along his spine were thousands of tiny polyps, erupting one after another. The structural integrity of his body was quickly breaking down. His skin tore open like cheesecloth. Muscles slipped off bone. Chunks of flesh turned instantly necrotic before sloughing off. He was in pain, but he didn't struggle. Brad became a puddle of mud. A quagmire dissolving into smaller and smaller parts. Sinking into the soil. Into the earth. A hundred billion corpses lead the way, and now Brad was one of them.

The newlyweds waited until the birds started chirping again before they turned back around to face their stone castle. Stepping over the hallowed ground where Brad disappeared. All they wanted to do was get on with their lives. They didn't ask for any of this. They didn't even ask to be born in the first place.

Myles grabbed the handle, but Elenya reached out, staying his hand for a moment. A look of worry on her porcelain face.

"Should we be doing this?" she asked.

"This is what we wanted, isn't it?" Myles replied.

Elenya took a deep breath and nodded. Okay. Yes. Myles was right. This is what she wanted. And they hadn't fought this hard not to see this thing all the way through.

Myles twisted the knob and the two of them stepped inside.

FINAL NIGHT

AND
THESE
FOOTSTEPS
WILL
ECHO
LONG
AFTER
WE'RE
GONE

XVII

And then there were footsteps.

Light and limber against the floorboards. It was the sound of their footsteps. The newlyweds entered the familiar-looking room.

Boxes were stacked up in towers around them. Elenya's handwriting scribbled across the sides in permanent black marker. STATIONERY and TOWELS and ASSORTED KITCHEN STUFF. It didn't take them long to recognize the place.

"What is this?" asked Myles, though he already knew the answer.

"Oh shit. We're back in the apartment. This is all our stuff."

On the coffee table sat their old copy of *Don Quixote*, restored.

"All our stuff is back. Just like it was our first night," he said. "We spent all day dragging these boxes in, remember? This is exactly where we left them. Same order and everything. We jumped backward three days."

"What?" Elenya squeaked. "Why? How?"

"Fucked if I know," Myles replied. "But I ain't about to stick around here an' deal with this same ole bullshit all over again. We already know how it goes. An' I'm done. So c'mon. Let's get back outside. Before we get trapped again."

Myles spun around and tried to reopen the front door. It wouldn't budge. He tried again. Twisted as hard as he could. It was like the handle was glued in place.

"Oh no."

Already starting to panic, Myles ran his hands along the frame, looking for some kind of weakness or vulnerable point. He clawed at all the cracks, trying to unscrew the screws. But it was no use. Mildew was already starting to form in his wake. Everywhere he touched suddenly turned green. The white fuzz quickly formed on top. The first stages of growth for their homespun fungus. Soon they would suppurate. Soon they would rot.

He tried the window next. Same results. Now he was panicking even more.

Myles ran around the apartment, checking everywhere he could think of where there might have been a breach. Even in the most illogical of places. Flushing the toilet. Opening and closing the closet doors. Stomping across this familiar terrain.

"Myles, stop! You're making it worse."

"What are you talking about?"

"Look at where you touched. The mold is crusting over. You're resealing us in."

"Me?! What about you, Ellie? Why don'tcha look at where you're stepping?"

Elenya looked at the footprints she left on the floor. Tufts of mold were growing out of them, in all the spots her moist skin patted against the freshly-lacquered wood. Her mouth dropped open. The entire living room was infested. And they'd only been here a few minutes.

"Oh no . . . " she said, her voice trembling. "No, no, no."

"This doesn't make sense," said Myles. "I thought we were cured."

She could feel her adrenaline pumping. Her heart beat so hard in her chest that it drowned everything else out. She walked past Myles and made her way toward their bedroom at the end of the hall. She knew she wasn't going to like what she was going to find in there. But she peeked in anyway.

She saw herself. Lying in bed in the darkness. Eyes open. Chest rising in and out. She rolled over. Myles slept next to her. She gave him a shake.

"Myles wake up, there's someone else in here . . . "

Oh shit. Oh shit. This was impossible.

Elenya ran back down the hallway and grabbed Myles by the shoulders.

"It's us," she shouted.

"What?"

"Me and you. We're already here. In the bedroom."

"You're not making any sense."

"Don't you get it? It was us the whole time. All those bumps in the night. They were our footsteps. We were haunting ourselves."

"Ellie . . ."

"Shut up and listen. I can hear you. The OTHER you. The OLD you, from days ago. Getting out of bed. I can hear the two of us bickering. You were skeptical. Remember. You said I was hearing things. You said it was nothing. But we searched the entire apartment anyway. Here you come now. Down the hallway. Turning on the light."

Click.

The lights turned on and Elenya and Myles both disappeared. *Poof.* Winked out of existence. It was not unlike being anesthetized. How the world suddenly went away, replaced by yawning endless nothingness. Until it was over. In this case, when the other version of them turned the lights off again and went back to bed.

Click.

Elenya and Myles returned as abruptly as they'd vanished. The lights went out and then *poof* they were back from the void.

"What the FUCK was THAT?!" shouted Myles, hands out to his sides like he was trying to keep his balance. He gulped so loudly even Elenya could hear it.

"We were the ghosts," she said. "We disappeared in the light."

"Oh my god, I'm not a fuckin' ghost, Ellie. I'm not even dead."

"Yeah. You're right. So maybe we're not ghosts then. Maybe we're something else. Something NEW."

"Like what?"

She looked down at the mold sprouting out of their footprints. Already spreading to the boxes. Up the sides of the couch. She raised her eyebrow. Gave it a nod.

Myles shook his head. "So what are you saying, Ellie? That somehow *we're* the mold? That we sealed up our own door? That we infected ourselves?"

Sunrise suddenly interrupted their discussion.

And the two of them once again vanished.

And all was silent.

And then, after midnight, it was silent no more.

Elenya and Myles reappeared in the living room nearly eighteen hours later. Though, from their perspective, the trip was almost instantaneous. Time was softening around them. The past and future and present no longer felt so concrete, though they couldn't escape the feeling that things were somehow circling the drain.

"Jeezus Christ, why does that keep happening!?" Myles shouted.

"My guess would be that the mold prefers the darkness," Elenya replied. "I'm not an expert or anything, but isn't that the case? Mold and mildews tend to proliferate in places where it's dark and cold and fall dormant in places where it's warm and bright."

"Oh so I'm *proliferating* now?"

"I would say so, Myles. Look around. It's only the second night here, and things have already degraded so fast. And it's not just the floors and the walls anymore either. Take a look at your arm. It's like you're being replaced."

Myles looked down and could see through his skin to the floor. Through their feet. Throughout their entire bodies. Thousands of tendrils were woven together. The mycelium was inside of him, filling his veins with mildew, taking the shape of his limbs from within. Except now, it felt different. Ameliorative. The mold wasn't trying to rot him apart but put him back together. Repairing. Replacing. Reconstituting. Oh lord. And a soporific sense of calm accompanied this physical change, not altogether unpleasant. It was rather peaceful, in fact.

His skin seemed to glow, veins shining through. Wispy and white. Indeed, at a glance, he looked like a ghost.

He took a sharp breath to try to clear his head. Whatever was inside of him was clouding his thoughts. He fought back and refused to give in. He knew he'd never figure any of this out if he gave in. He had to fight it. He and Elenya were running out of time.

"I'm gonna go see if I can talk to us. The OTHER us. We have to get them out of here, Ellie. It's the only hope we have if you want any kind of future other than this."

"Myles . . . " she reached out, but he was stomping down the hallway into the bedroom, where he found the Elenya from their second night. He loomed over her, trying to explain the situation. Trying to pass on some knowledge that might change how this was all bound to play out. Their future. His past. Their present. Wherever they were.

Of course, it didn't seem to matter what he said. She didn't seem to understand him. They were two different species speaking two different languages. The Elenya from the past merely laid there beneath him. Half-terrified. Half-asleep. Unable to hear him. Unable to help herself.

Defeated, Myles returned to the living room. Elenya nodded sympathetically. She recalled the night well, though now it seemed barely more than a dream.

"I thought you were the foreman of a construction crew," she told him. "We were already starting to rot and it was already out of my mind. It seems so foolish now that I'm on the other end. I thought you were going to build me a castle. I had always wanted to live in a castle."

Myles nodded sadly.

"I know."

Sunrise. Sunset. It was like she blinked and the room around them was once again covered in fungus. Rotted completely to pieces. The putrid black spot in the center, almost ready to split wide open and swallow them whole.

Of course this time, Elenya and Myles had no reason to fear it. They'd explored the darkness from every angle they could. They confronted the future and eventually, let go. They didn't need to understand things in order to accept them. And they didn't need to accept things in order to understand them.

The mushrooms woke up. Unfurling, they reached out like thousands of little hands trapped in the sludge, beckoning them home. But before they could answer, there came a sound behind them. The DeNovas spun around to see Elenya—the OTHER Elenya—standing on the far side of the room. Their wedding picture fell off the wall.

"This is it," said Elenya. "The last time I saw us. This is our final moment. After this, we disappear into a place where we won't return."

"So we can't help them?" Myles felt a twinge of panic. A shiver of regret. Though these feelings didn't last long. The mold soothed him. Everything was exactly how it should be. How it always had been.

"Well, there's one thing I can do," said Elenya.

"What?"

"I can show her how to get here. And then I can move on."

Elenya turned and faced her former self, already rotten to pieces.

She reached out and touched herself in the center of her own forehead. In an instant, she was transported to the place beyond death. It would be a long hard road for this other Elenya to get here, but she'd make it eventually. It was about as happy an ending as anyone could hope to have.

Elenya DeNova approached the black spot just an inch from the ends of her toes. This time, Myles stood next to her, and he took her by the hand in the same way he did on their first date all those years ago. Their arms outstretched wide like Christ the Redeemer. Like a pair of birds. The two of them on the edge of the precipice, overlooking the city. Overlooking the entire world. I'm flying, Elenya exclaimed with delight, though they both knew their feet were still planted firmly on the ground. But whatever.

In that moment, at least, anything seemed possible.

In that moment, at least, anything seemed possible.

ACKNOWLEDGEMENTS

Thank you to the following people who help me bring this book into the world in ways big and small: Constance Ann Fitzgerald, John Skipp, Max Booth III, Lori Michelle, Matt Blairstone, Alex Woodroe, Rose O'Keefe, Michael Allen Rose, and of course, my shitty old landlord, who rented me the shitty old apartment around which I built this story.

ABOUT THE CONTRIBUTORS

Danger Slater is the Wonderland Award-winning writer of *I Will Rot Without You, Moonfellows, He Digs a Hole*, and other books too. He has a mustache. Or maybe he shaved it by now. Or maybe he is already dead. I don't know when you're reading this.

Kate Blairstone makes pictures about Identity, using cultural detritus, plants and animals as symbols for people, places and ideas. Kate works from her home studio in Portland, Oregon, where she lives with her husband, six-year-old son and two pesky cats. More at www.kateblairstone.com.

Echo Echo is a Portuguese artist and a proponent of *horror vacui:* an aversion to leaving empty spaces in her artwork. She immerses herself in individual pieces for up to a year at a time and renders in extreme detail. Echo also performs in multiple bands, finding equal freedom in expressing herself through music as she does through illustration.

ABOUT TENEBROUS PRESS

Tenebrous Press was conceived in the Plague Year 2020 and unleashed, howling and feral, in spring 2021 to deliver the finest in transgressive, progressive Horror from diverse and unsung voices around the world.

We welcome the esoteric; the unorthodox; the finest in New Weird Horror.

FIND OUT MORE:
www.tenebrouspress.com
Twitter: @TenebrousPress

NEW WEIRD HORROR